The Bitcoin Revolution:
Following the Money

By P. Carl Mullan

MW00955660

Copyright © 2014 by Philip Carl Mullan

All rights reserved. This book or any portion thereof may not be reproduced or used in any manner whatsoever without the express written permission of the publisher except for the use of brief quotations in a book review.

Bitcoin is a new innovative version of electronic cash and has many of the same features of physical cash. For those without access to conventional banking services, Bitcoin has proven to be a beneficial asset.

However, pseudonymous Bitcoin has also become one of the preferred methods of payment used by today's Internet criminals.

While Bitcoin moves through the blockchain advancing freedom around the world, it also enables a great deal of online criminal activities. With any digital "cash" product, it is impossible to have the good without the bad.

While this is a fictional tale, it is based on actual situations, people and events from today's headlines. The story also illustrates some of the flawed actions taken by government agents and prosecutors as they attempt to curtail illegal Bitcoin activity.

In today's info-apocalypse world, those seeking to destroy another person's reputation will connect them with terrorism, child pornography, money laundering or drugs. This statement rings true throughout the past decade of digital currency media coverage. These are the four horsemen of the info-apocalypse.

This book loosely follows Bitcoin users as their currency moves through the blockchain. These stories provide graphic real life examples of who is using Bitcoin, what business is being conducted through the blockchain, and some not so obvious reasons why people choose virtual currency over conventional bank products.

All of these fictional stories were created from real life events and situations. The characters, places and events detailed on these pages provide a glimpse into one possible future version Bitcoin in the United States.

All characters appearing in this work are fictitious. Any resemblance to real persons, living or dead, is purely coincidental.

Table of Contents

Contents

Part 1 8

   Seattle, Washington 8

   Beverly Hills, California...11

   Beijing, China 14

   Southeast Portland, Oregon 15

   Great Falls, South Carolina..17

   Denver, Colorado..19

   Raqqa, Syria...21

   Pearl District, Portland, Oregon...23

   Beijing, China 25

   Seattle, Washington 25

   Melbourne, Australia 26

   Santa Clarita, California 28

   Burbank, California 31

   Raqqa, Syria...32

   Denver, Colorado..34

   Location Unknown 36

Part 2 38

   Portland, Oregon..38

   Raqqa, Syria...41

   Seattle, Washington 42

   West Africa...44

   Burbank, California 45

   Denver, Colorado..47

   Location Unknown 48

   Beverly Hills, California...49

Denver, Colorado...53

Burgas, Bulgaria 54

Atlanta, Georgia...57

Moscow, Russian Federation...60

Denver, Colorado...65

Raqqa, Syria...66

Location Unknown 68

Melbourne, Australia 69

Moscow, Russian Federation...69

Part 3 72

Atlanta, Georgia...72

Louisville, Kentucky..73

Beverly Hills, California...77

Tel Aviv, Israel 77

Lagos, Nigeria..83

Raqqa, Syria...84

Moscow, Russian Federation...85

Seattle, Washington 88

Portland, Oregon..93

Great Falls, South Carolina..93

Pearl District Portland, Oregon.......................................94

Atlanta, Georgia...97

Louisville, Kentucky..98

Tel Aviv, Israel 99

Seattle, Washington 101

Buenes Aries, Argentina...102

Portland, Oregon..103

Buenes Aries, Argentina...107

Pearl District Portland, Oregon.....................................108

5

Part 4 110

  Lagos, Nigeria..110

  Great Falls, South Carolina.............................112

  Beverly Hills, California.................................113

  Seattle, Washington 116

  Southeast Portland, Oregon 119

  Santa Clarita, California 120

  Lagos, Nigeria..121

  Seattle, Washington 122

  West Africa..122

  Santa Clarita, California 124

  Seattle, Washington 127

  Santa Clarita, California 129

  Burbank, California 131

  The Federal Government & Operation Rocket..........132

  Denver, Colorado..134

  Melbourne, Australia 135

  Denver, Colorado..136

Heralded by an angel as bringing death, famine, war, and conquest unto man, these are the four horsemen of the apocalypse as depicted in a woodcut by Albrecht Dürer circa 1498.

In today's digital world, the four horseman of the info-apocalypse are terrorism, child pornography, money laundering, and drugs. …And behold a white horse.

Part 1

<u>Seattle, Washington</u>
Julia was now 28 years old and living with her longtime boyfriend
Steven just outside of Seattle. 6 months earlier, her dream of
completing college had died, and she was simply trying to pay the
bills and keep her head above water. That is when she was first
introduced to Bitcoin.

She and Steven had been living in one-half of a duplex, located in a
safe, but inexpensive neighborhood about 20 minutes from
downtown Seattle. The neighborhood had been built in the late
1960s. Most of their neighbors avoided lawn care, in favor of gravel,
moss and the ever present broken down car. The houses were
livable, cheap, and all the couple could afford when they had moved
in two years ago.

In the past six months, both of their lives had drastically changed.
Now working from home, they shared the job title of Bitcoin miner.
With the price of Bitcoin virtual currency climbing to over $100 a
coin, she and Steven had become full-time miners. Over the past six
months, they had been buying equipment and continuously mining
Bitcoin. The smallest profit the couple had earned was $1200 after
their first month.

As Bitcoin prices rose, and more people around the world began
using cryptocurrency, Bitcoin mining had emerged as a very
lucrative new industry.

Steven had been a line cook at a local seafood restaurant for the past
nine years. He had recently given up that career in favor of Bitcoin
mining. Each new month the couple's mining profits had been
steadily rising. In the last 30 days, they had cleared over $3800 in
profit. Julia considered buying a new car or at least a new-used one.

Steven loved not having to wake up early and go into work each day.
They both agreed; the new "Bitcoin miner" lifestyle was nothing
short of fabulous. Julia felt like a technology guru. She believed that
Bitcoin mining was helping to make a positive impact on the world.

By mining Bitcoins, they were strengthening a new decentralized platform that could ultimately help virtual currency become a mainstream method of payment. As she brewed a fresh cup of chamomile tea, she thought, "What an amazing time to be alive."

Julia's background in computers afforded her a full technical understanding of the Bitcoin mining process. Steven, however, never fully grasped the innovation born from the Bitcoin blockchain. He didn't comprehend how solving powerful mathematical problems allowed all of the Byzantine generals to attack the fort at the same time.

Fortunately, Julia had the knowledge and computer experience that led them to the building and set-up of their powerful Bitcoin home mining rigs. Steven was left with the responsibility of continuously supervising the profitable operation that now occupied their living room.

They both attended the weekly local Bitcoin Meetups where they sold most of their newly mined coins. Occasionally, they offered some Bitcoins online through the popular website MyLocalBitcoins.net and received a bank wire or EFT. A few times Julia had sold some coins through popular exchanges in China. However, bank payments in exchange for Bitcoin were very rare. They both viewed Bitcoin mining as a cash business, and that's the way Julia wanted to keep it. She was still wrestling with an overdue student loan, and there were creditors calling every week chasing down Steven's overdue bills. Julia believed that Bitcoin was the new digital cash. It was an electronic representation of cash currency and no bank was needed to function in the Bitcoin universe. She wanted to keep the government out of their Bitcoin finance.

The tiny house was now packed with computers and mining rigs. The living room was lined with faded blue plastic shelving units from Walmart. Using plastic shelves was essential with the exposed wiring and electrical parts that make up the mining rigs.

Since the electronic components and the cheap plastic shelves were both lightweight, the shelves had also been secured to the interior living room walls with small, colorful sections of used bungee cord.

In front of each shelving unit sat the "guts" of each mining rig. The "guts" usually included a Raspberry Pi, a hulking power supply, and piles of wiring that linked it all together. The expensive graphics boards using for mining sat side-by-side on each plastic shelf. Noisy cooling fans also ran on each shelf whirling away throughout the day and the night. Tiny LED lights feverishly blinked as they peeked out from behind congested circuit boards. At night, the tall shelves with their thick cables streaming down to the floor reminded Steven of that scary Slender Man character.

Several laptops also inhabited the plastic shelves. These monitored the rigs and kept track of mining speeds, power supply units, hash rates, electrical consumption and overall mining statistics.

There were certain obstacles to Bitcoin mining. The first drawback was that mining required a massive amount of electrical power. Each mining rig needed around 1000 watts of power and a few of the newer units required even more. The lonely breaker box that regulated power to their side of the duplex was maxed out.

When all of the equipment and the air conditioners were running, the main breaker would sometimes blow. Julie had tried washing clothes while the two air conditioners were on and had blown out the whole house. The same thing happened while vacuuming.

After the first two major outages, tiny pink Post-it® Notes had appeared stuck to all of the major appliances reminding both of them to turn off the air conditioning before proceeding with that appliance.

The electric bills had been averaging about $2300 a month for the past four months, but the Bitcoin mining had still proven to be very lucrative. The cost, of powering all the mining units, was Bitcoin drawback number one.

The second major drawback was the heat and noise. There were two full-time AC window units in the living room which helped cool the mining rigs. These units ran full time and were a major contributor to the noise level. Each of the graphics boards also had a cooling fan and some used several fans per board. These additional noise makers buzzed along 24/7 creating a sound like a tiny tornado whirling around the living room.

In an ongoing attempt to solve the noise problem, Julia had collected old egg cartons that now covered the walls and ceilings. She thought it looked remarkably similar to Christian Bale's Bat cave in The Dark Knight Rises. Most of the windows were also covered in thick black poster board, with egg cartons taped over them. It was not attractive, but the cartons were very functional in lowering the noise.

The interior of the cozy residence was now dark, hot and noisy, but the couple had never been happier.

On July 8th, Bitcoin miners, Julia, and Steven, discovered a new block of Bitcoin and they were awarded another 50 coins.

Beverly Hills, California

> Spouses are becoming more creative in their attempts to hide marital assets during California Civil Divorce proceedings. Because a divorce is one-half of all family assets, husbands are going to immense lengths to protect wealth prior to the asset disclosure process.

> ~Fred Arnett, Attorney at Santa Barbara Family Law Center

Larry softly closed the carved mahogany doors to his home office situated on the lower level of the family's lavish Bel Air estate. He paused for a moment, thinking about his young wife loitering around upstairs with their new son. As this was the phone call to begin divorce proceedings, he questioned whether he should leave the estate and call from their Malibu house.

Moments later, he firmly picked up the desk phone and hit speed dial number 1, connecting him with the office of his longtime friend and prominent Beverly Hills attorney, Bernie Levine.

"Lawrence Evans calling for Mr. Levine. No, Celia, he's not expecting my call, thank you." He said into the phone.

As he waited, he wondered how painful Bernie's response would be as Larry announced the start of divorce number three. After his vicious split with wife number two, Larry was likely to endure a mountain of grief and I-told-you-so from Bernie. The split with wife number two had been categorized by the law office as, "the most expensive event of Larry's entire life."

Hearing the familiar sound of Bernie picking up the line, Larry decided to speak first. He said "Bernie, I'm going to take you up on your offer…. What offer? Don't you remember, after that expensive split with wife number two, you promised me half off on my next divorce. Yes, it's that time again, damn it. Little David is up and walking, let's get her out of here." Staring down at the floor, Larry let out a deep breath, began lightly kicking his desk and put the call on speaker.

Larry, or Lawrence as he is known in the film community, was second generation Hollywood royalty. In the mid-1960's, his father had taken a small studio, loaded it with a string of blockbuster hits and created the third richest film business in America. After Larry took over the company, he had battled the advent of VHS and was successful in continuing his father's profitable film legacy.

Now 56 years old, nothing moved in Hollywood without his first look. Although Larry was approaching his third failed marriage, he felt very confident about his career and the film empire he would someday leave his new son David.

The new wife, just 32 years old, was a former dancer and aspiring actress. Their son David was Larry's fourth child and only boy. He had been born just seven months after their couple's quickie Malibu wedding. The child's early birth was no surprise to anyone that knew Larry.

Recognizing that the best law firms around town would happily represent wife number three in this legal proceeding, both Larry and Bernie understood it could be a costly event if Larry did not begin consolidating his assets.

Bernie's voice was now heard through the speakerphone, "Larry, I can't advise you on the financial aspects of this divorce, other than to say number three will get half of what her lawyers can find. Have you heard of Bitcoin?"

Larry responded, "Just what I see in the newspaper."

Bernie continued, "A lot of my clients have been taking advantage of investments in Bitcoin, prior to any asset search. The invested funds disappear into this digital currency virtual universe and re-emerge a year or three down the road. It's untraceable, and no one is the wiser. If number three's team didn't locate the funds in their initial searches, it would not appear on the asset list. It is very simple to convert money into Bitcoin; it's not like precious metals that require storage in a bank box. I'm sure her attorneys will seek to open any bank boxes with your name on them. Bitcoins can be hidden away on any memory device such as a thumb drive or even a tiny SD card. Money that is stored in digital cryptocurrency can't be located by anyone, including the government. Plus, it is fast and simple to convert it back to dollars at any time. Larry are you listening to me?"

Larry says, "Yes, Bernie, I'm listening."

Bernie continues to talk on speaker, "You didn't hear this from me, and I mention it only because some of our firm's other clients, facing similar proceedings, have had success protecting their cash assets through investments in Bitcoin. I seem to remember, from divorce number two, do you remember, it was the most expensive event in your life. You had twenty-six bank accounts, and only five of them were jointly owned. Larry, Bitcoin is proper protection, it works and I think that you could use some additional help in this area. When we go to file, Larry, I don't want to see any significant balances in those accounts do you understand?"

Larry confirmed, "Yes, I believe I understand, but I don't know anything about this Bitcoin thing."

"I work with a legal and accounting professional here in town, for these types of investments. I'll have Celia make an appointment for you with our accountant Todd Smith, at Allen, Smith and Cohen, Professional Accountants and Financial Advisors. Are you still there Larry? Are you listening to me Larry? I want you to go see Todd, and he will fix you up for any Bitcoin transactions you need. He's a Bitcoin expert, and Todd is a professional. Larry you can speak with him in total confidence."

Beijing, China

After just two years of continuous studying, Peter had voluntarily withdrawn from Beijing's Tsinghua University in favor of a position at a nearby blossoming local startup company. The company, called BTC-Beijing, traded Bitcoin and also produced software products such as mobile Bitcoin wallets and point-of-sales merchant software.

Peter was a software engineer and designer. During year one, the process of creating new Bitcoin software, had been especially challenging for the start-up company. However, lately, the company's efforts were paying off. The BTC-Beijing online wallet had become the most famous Bitcoin product of its kind in all of Asia. BTC-Beijing now serviced more than one million online wallets for global customers. Peter's software developed into a new closed system of trading Bitcoin "in-house". Peter referred to this process as an "off-market" transaction. It was a new digital currency company ledger that allowed Bitcoin value to move between accounts within the existing business network.

Peter's focus had been on creating a direct in-house connection for those one million current BTC-Beijing customers, which would allow them to execute off-market Bitcoin transactions. In-house operations also meant that no record of the transfer would ever appear in the Bitcoin blockchain.

The two cryptocurrency obstacles that Peter's new software addressed were Bitcoin confirmation times and transaction fees. In all Bitcoin transactions, as the value moves between Bitcoin wallets, that movement needs to be confirmed by other participants in the network. Once confirmation by other peers in the system has taken place, the transaction becomes permanent. Merchants had required around six confirmations before a transfer was pronounced permanent or complete. This delay, waiting for multiple confirmations often took several minutes or longer. A sales delay could become a negative issue for certain retail operations. Using Peter's new system, the transactions were not subject to waiting or uncertainty. Not requiring any confirmations, these transactions settled instantly and some customers considered this to be a significant advantage.

The Bitcoin transaction fee is an incentive on the part of a Bitcoin user to ensure that miners included particular transactions in the next newly created block in the Bitcoin blockchain. For most individual transactions, a fee is required and for some it is voluntary. Using Peter's in-house system, there were never any transaction fees. In-house trading allowed Bitcoins to flow effortlessly, instantly and cost free through all accounts at BTC-Beijing.

He had also developed a very effective mobile app for this platform that was widely accepted by users across Asia. Transactions on Peter's mobile app also cleared instantly, were free to BTC-Beijing clients and never appeared in the Bitcoin blockchain.

The app became an instant hit with local users and soon translated into extensive global use. Many Chinese used this app just like a Bitcoin ATM. Anyone could sell coins in person for cash and transfer the units instantly from their account into the retail customers' accounts.

Southeast Portland, Oregon

The Main Street Bakery had been operating in SE Portland for 29 years. Paul and Sarina, the couple who owned the business, were some of the original "hippies" who immigrated to Portland's now famous Southeast over 30 years ago. The bakery business was very popular, and the company regularly supported the local community.

Success had led them to open two additional locations, one downtown and one in the Pearl District.

The Main Street Bakery employed twelve people full-time and four part-time drivers. They delivered baked goods to just about every popular restaurant and hotel in town. Many of the busy food trucks also purchased buns and breads from the bakery each day.

Paul had discovered Bitcoin in 2010 and bought 500 at a price of .01 cent each. That same year, they also began accepting Bitcoin in the bakery. The first year had not yielded many cryptocurrency transactions, but during the summer of 2012, it seemed like everyone in Portland began to talk about Bitcoin. These days, the currency was accepted all over town at locally owned shops, restaurants, and businesses.

The only issue for Paul and Sarina was the often wild fluctuations in Bitcoin's market price. The price would sometimes move up or down $20-40 per day. For a bakery operating at a small profit, this type of downward movement in Bitcoin's price could wipe out the bakery's profit margin.

If Paul held on to the bakery's Bitcoins more than 3-4 days, by the time the he exchanged the coins into dollars, the slim profit generated through bakery sales might be lost in the currency swap. Paul thought to himself, "Any business that holds on to Bitcoin was taking a risk the price might move lower. Any small business owner was perhaps risking the loss of their profit margin."

In late summer, Paul's Bitcoin price issue was solved. That September, a new US company operating out of San Francisco had opened called BitStarter. This new business acted as a merchant service and an instant Bitcoin exchange. It offered very low-cost merchant processing and instant exchange from Bitcoin to cash.

The bakery could sell all of their delicious treats for Bitcoins, and Bitstarter would pay them each day in dollars. If a loaf of bread costs $12.00 and Paul accepted Bitcoins, at the end of the day he would see $12.00 of cash in his bank account. He never even handled the Bitcoins, so it was a win-win situation for his business.

BitStarter took all the worry and price risk out of accepting Bitcoin as a merchant. Both he and Sarina were very pleased with the new service. At present, they were taking in $200 to $300 in Bitcoin sales each day. Using BitStarter, all of those funds were now automatically sent each day into their Rivermark Credit Union account.

Great Falls, South Carolina

> There is no crueler tyranny than that which is perpetuated under the shield of law and in the name of justice.
>
> ~Charles de Montesquieu

There was only one large indoor shopping mall near Great Falls, South Carolina. The well air-conditioned mall contained three national brand name department stores, one large sporting goods outlet, 34 small retailers and a busy food court. Charlie visited the mall each Saturday. Being at the mall, particularly the food court, made him feel safe. He enjoyed all of the people and sounds that moved about him as he walked. The mall created a warm kind of environment Charlie enjoyed.

Traveling to the mall was easy. Charlie took the number 4 public bus with the number 15, which then dropped him off just steps from the mall's food court entrance. Once inside, he went directly to the Hot Dog Hut for his favorite meal, a foot long and waffle fries. He loved the waffle fries.

For Charlie, the Saturday mall trip was a weekly pilgrimage. Since his new job had started at the Walmart, and he began collecting weekly paychecks, Charlie could afford to visit the food court every weekend. This bus trip had taken place each week for the past eight years. The only Saturday he had missed was when the mall closed for Hurricane Agnes, and even then he had showed up but could not get inside.

Today's mall visit was special, because, Charlie's Walmart supervisor was having a birthday soon. James was his Walmart boss, however, in keeping with store policy, he had asked Charlie always to refer to him as a "supervisor" and not boss man.

While deciding what birthday gift to buy his supervisor, he had discovered a 20% off coupon for one of the large department stores in the mall. That Saturday, Charlie had planned on using the discount and buying James a fancy new tie.

As the weekend rolled around, Charlie found himself finishing off a foot long dog and strolling over to the department store.

The clerk scanned Charlie's tie selection, and the cash register displayed $18.23, as Charlie slid his only credit card through the reader.

That card was Charlie's pride and joy. Earlier this year, the bank had his raised his limit up to a full $500. This new level was more than double his original $200 limit. He was very proud of his banking skills and that one card.

As the cashier completed the sale, Charlie almost forgot to give him the 20% coupon.

Moments later, the clerk smiled and said, "Thank you, Mr. Martin, please shop with us again." Briefly acknowledging the comment, Charlie strolled away with his boss's new birthday gift.

Charlie grew up being told he was born with Intellectual disability (ID), and as a kid, everyone had called him a retard. At a very early age, the State of South Carolina had become his legal guardian and throughout his childhood had confined him to an institution.

After turning 19, he had transitioned out of the institution and into a halfway house. Two years later, he moved into his current one bedroom apartment. Now, almost 30, Charlie was a well-liked part of the Great Falls community. He worked at the nearby Walmart for over eight years and always made sure to reference his store as "the Walmart" because his town only had one Walmart location. The lifelong disability, which had plagued Charlie as a child, was later diagnosed with a type of Asperger syndrome.

Denver, Colorado

Located throughout Denver's metropolitan area, Mr. Green's Dispensary, had operated as a legal Medical Marijuana Dispensary for many years. With the recent legalization of pot in Colorado, Mr. Green's had become a Recreational Marijuana Dispensary, providing local customers with accessible, top quality cannabis in a friendly and professional environment.

Mr. Green's welcomed all public clients, over 21, and the store no longer required a red card.

Colorado's new legal marijuana business was experiencing some start-up financial headaches caused by old Federal Government Regulations and Uncle Sam's tight hold on the US banking system. Unfortunately, while the State of Colorado said it was "ok" to legally sell pot, Marijuana remained illegal under federal law. Enacted in 1970 by the federal government, The Controlled Substances Act still classified marijuana as a Schedule I drug. US banks and payment processing companies were very cognizant of the federal regulations and were unwilling to risk providing financial services for this new industry.

Apparently, almost all US states were still in agreement with Uncle Sam regarding the apparent dangers of other Schedule I drugs. However, the country's recession and a shrinking local tax base had caused Colorado State Representatives to change their opinion of pot and begin viewing marijuana as just another harmless taxable over-the-counter intoxicant. It's worth noting, that while many other states permit the sale of medical marijuana, no US state had yet attempted to legalize any other federal Schedule I drug such heroin, LSD or ecstasy.

The country's outdated regulatory patchwork of state and federal laws forced banks dealing with the new marijuana laws, including state-chartered ones into a tight corner. The legacy of US banking had left the entire Colorado financial services community, fearing enforcement of federal statutes that could punish them for providing services to legal marijuana businesses.

Even entrepreneurs that had tried using their personal bank accounts for the legal pot business found their accounts flagged because of excessive cash deposits and closed by the bank's compliance department.

The big name credit card companies that mainly operated out of Delaware, a state where pot sales are still very much illegal, would not allow their financial platforms for processing these type of payments. Consequently, any legal new pot business in Colorado was left to handle all sales using cash.

Additionally, no bank would loan the new legal Colorado industry any startup capital. Georgina, the owner of Mr. Green's Dispensary, had been forced to borrow $1.2 million dollars, as a personal loan, from old friends in California.

The government was still in bed the nation's banking industry. Until the federal government changed its old 1970's laws, there would be no bank transactions, no bank loans, and no credit card processing for Colorado's new legal industry.

The other headache, caused by federal regulations, came from the Internal Revenue Service (IRS).

The IRS required all businesses to pay quarterly taxes by bank wire (electronically). Mr. Green's Dispensary, which was unable to open a US bank account, found it impossible to send a bank wire. Consequently, legal marijuana businesses, without bank accounts, were being unfairly fined a 10 percent penalty on federal employee withholding taxes because the companies were unable to submit payment on time using a bank wire. Without a bank account, Mr. Green's operation was being fined each quarter by the IRS. Additionally, Mr. Green's had to pay the quarterly tax payments using bulk cash, and that was no easy task. There was only one IRS office in Colorado, which accepted cash payments and a meeting with those IRS agents, was only by appointment.

The owner and operators of Mr. Green's were aggressively looking for new financial solutions, when Bitcoin fell into their lap. The prior week, 4 Denver area locations of Mr. Green's Dispensary, had received new electronic marijuana vending machines for use in the stores.

These machines could drastically cut down on customer wait times and also provided shoppers with a new convenient electronic method of payment called Bitcoin virtual currency. Bitcoin was a non-governmental currency and not legal tender. The banks had no control over Bitcoin, and anyone could use it.

A Bitcoin payment was also non-repudiable. This phrase, which was originally made famous by e-gold.com in the 1990's, defined the outcome of an online digital currency payment. Regarding cryptocurrency, a non-repudiable payment would mean that no one could stop any Bitcoin user from sending funds to any other account, and no Bitcoin account could block anyone from receiving an incoming payment. Once a Bitcoin transaction was confirmed, it was irrevocable and irreversible.

Bitcoin payments traveled outside of conventional banking platforms and in some cases the payments were even anonymous. The secure non-bank owned payment system that permitted very inexpensive fund transfers around the world was the ideal solution for Colorado's new marijuana businesses.

Georgina Ray, the owner of Mr. Green's, considered Bitcoin to be a dynamic version of electronic cash. This new decentralized payment system as an ideally suited method-of-payment for her company's products. She envisioned a future Denver Post byline might read, "Mr. Green's: First US company to sell marijuana from Bitcoin enabled vending machines." In her eyes, Bitcoin was a total financial solution for this new industry. She quietly said to herself, "Banks! We don't need no stinking banks!"

Raqqa, Syria

> By circumventing the world's financial system and adding a layer of anonymity to transactions, Bitcoin has changed the way that threat financing is structured for global jihad networks.

~US Naval Services Strategy Report: Combating the Flow of
Terror Funding, US Naval Research Laboratory, Threat
Assessment Task Force

Educated in the United States at an Ivy League school, Amir now sat
in the basement of a reinforced shelter located on the captured
military airport of Raqqa, Syria. The western education and degree
in media studies had earned him the position of media consultant for
the Islamic State. An FBI report described him as, "Educated with a
college degree related to computer technology and previously
employed by a media relations & telecommunications company."
A few years ago, he had worked very effectively as part of the
"media wing" for al-Qaeda in Iraq (AQI), which then evolved into
the Islamic State.

Amir had been responsible for leveraging his computer skills in
order to spread the group's propaganda across the Internet using
social media. He referred to his program as the "The Islamic State's
Social Media Blitz" and this campaign had very successfully
energized their base.
Early in the campaign, he focused on the fact that the media,
particularly social media, could multiply the perception of their
organization's power around the world. He further tried to show that
the social message that followed an act of terror was sometimes as
important as the violence itself.

Several times, Amir had also been responsible for sending funds to
various new recruits drawn to the organization by his media
campaign.

Amir knew and understood Bitcoin very well. He had been
transferring funds to terror associates in African nations for almost a
year. Those Bitcoins had been used to support the process of signing
up new recruits.

In all of these cases, Bitcoin had functioned exceptionally well as an
anonymous method of sending money anywhere in the world.
Additionally, Bitcoin was already well known and widely used in

Kenya and Nigeria. There was a collective willingness of affiliates from African nations, with previous mobile payment experience, to accept and transact business with Bitcoin digital currency. 83 successful Bitcoin transfers to associates in African countries during the past year had solidified Amir's belief in virtual currency and sparked his interest in Bitcoin as a full-time method of funding the Islamic State.

Pearl District, Portland, Oregon

Brian's passion was producing high-quality wooden furniture from recycled hardwoods native to the Pacific Northwest. He was able to take logs that may have been cut for firewood and turn them into gorgeous interior natural furniture pieces suitable for a caring customer's home or office.

Brian's business manufactured and sold a unique line of natural wood furniture. The handcrafted pieces ranged from Siberian Elm Dinner tables, sourced from Scappoose, to a fantastic set of tables, carved out a 6 foot Fir slab rescued from a forest area in Mt. Tabor. He was very successful in his work and loved being a part of Portland's Artisan Economy.

His wife of 18 years was a licensed veterinarian who worked at nearby DoveLewis Emergency Animal Hospital.

Their only daughter, April had just turned 15. For the past year, he and his wife had been dispensing April's weekly allowance is Bitcoin. They both believed that someday, paper money would be replaced by digital currency and wanted their daughter prepared for the future as a "digital citizen".

At first, April had wanted to spend her Bitcoin at Target until it was explained to her that not every store accepted Bitcoin. This fact did not go over big with April. Mom then told her to find local merchants in the area that sold things she needed and not to spend money on imported crap from places like Target!

For that entire first month or so, April had pouted, and not spent any of her accumulated Bitcoin allowances. She then began searching online and reading posts by members of the Portland Bitcoin community. She found that Bitcoin could be used to purchase gift cards online which she could then use for shopping at local stores like Nike. With the first month's accumulated allowance now on a gift card, she and her dad visited the Official Nike store downtown on SW 5th Avenue. April purchased a very pink pair of Nike Free Express Girls' Running Shoes. Before leaving the location, she used the balance of her gift card buying a Nike Advantage Power Girls' Tennis Tank Top in brightly colored Fuchsia Force, also a bright pink color.

After a year of receiving Bitcoin, she pushed her dad to transfer the allowance each week. She had uncovered an online website that mapped out thousands of locations across the country and state that accepted Bitcoin. There were many shops in Portland and across Oregon on board the Bitcoin express!

Apparently, after seeing April's new Nike outfit, all of her friends at school also began using Bitcoin on their smartphones. Digital currency had become very popular with young adults. Many Portland parents triumphantly declared that a new feature, in addition to texting, had been discovered for a teenage girls's cell phone. The girls even accepted Bitcoin at all student bake sales.

Coincidentally, these high school age characters were the very same individuals skilled at hacking computers. While at school, April's mobile Bitcoin wallet had been compromised twice. Each time the sneaky student made off with all of her Bitcoins.

Brian had then taken a few minutes of quiet time and explained to April that unlike a credit card, a Bitcoin payment was not refundable. They could not get her Bitcoin's back or reverse the transaction. "No chargeback" was a big part of the new digital currency world. Brian had even discussed trying to track the school thief using the blockchain explorer and other such tools. However, they finally agreed to engage in some additional phone security and find a better way to store her phone.

Brian and his wife had been shopping online with Bitcoin for more than a year. They had found coffee shops and artisan local merchants around Portland that accepted the digital currency. April's mom declared that if a merchant produced local goods and accepted Bitcoin, their family should be shopping at that business.

Beijing, China

All of Peter's friends across China were excited this week, because, one of China's largest eCommerce conglomerates was going public, and the depository receipts would soon begin trading on the New York Stock Exchange. Peter and other employees of BTC-Beijing had the rare opportunity to buy this stock only moments after the public offering. Throughout the week, everyone, including Peter, had been selling Bitcoins and moving funds to brokerage accounts in order to take advantage of this once in a lifetime IPO opportunity.

Unfortunately, for Bitcoin, this created a wall of Chinese selling pressure. After just three days of Chinese selling, the price of Bitcoin had dropped more than $80 USD. Then today, it had moved another $20 USD lower. He hoped that the coming IPO would earn a healthy profit. However, he was also very concerned about a downward trend in Bitcoin's price.

Seattle, Washington

Julia and Steven were just arriving to the Satoshi Square Meetup in Seattle. They loved talking Bitcoins and were the last people to leave the occasion. However, tonight the couple was selling their freshly minted coins and needed to get busy talking with buyers. The Meetup took place in and around the Hard Rock Café in downtown Seattle. Tonight, the couple had 45 fresh Bitcoins they could sell, and there were bills to pay so this evening, they were not haggling over price.

Julie quickly found Noah, their regular buyer sitting at the bar, watching his laptop and talking on the mobile. In just a few minutes, Noah had purchased 45 coins and paid cash.

After completing a sale for their entire mining fortune, Julie and Steven were busy drinking beer and playing pool. As Steven leaned over the table to make his shot, he looked squarely up to Julia and asked, "You have all that cash on you correct? It's not in your purse; it's in your pocket right?" Julia grabbed the large pocket on the front of her overalls, smiled and responded, "It's on me like we do every month." She gently nodded her head then smiled affirming that it had been a successful and profitable night for the couple.

Melbourne, Australia

Abdul-Nur was his new Muslim name and just as it suggested; he was a faithful "servant of the light". Living in Melbourne, Australia, Abdul was a young tech-savvy man just 19 years of age who had been drawn to the jihad movement through information found online. The Jihadist English language online magazine, published by the Islamic State, had become his roadmap to the Middle East. The articles, advice, and photos had presented a very persuasive argument that moved him to take up the fight in Syria.

After studying computers at the local University, he understood encryption, proxy networks, and Internet privacy. He did not own a cell phone, nor did he want the authorities tracking him or listening in on his calls. This good advice for new recruits as found in Islamic State's online magazine.

Abdul thought to himself, "Westerners may consider this magazine propaganda, but this information has clarified my purpose and strengthened my resolve. Evidence found in these digital pages had justified my goal. I will take up arms."

The magazine even encouraged devoted readers to submit their material for publication. Abdul had been working on an article entitled, "Using Bitcoin to avoid detection," which he would present on his arrival in the Middle East.

As brand new recruits, Abdul and his three friends would soon be heading to Syria for training and front line fighting. From his online resources, they had learned the truth about Islam and now supported the ultimate goal of reestablishing an Islamic Caliphate.

Of the four new Australian recruits, Abdul had the most Internet experience. For more than two years, he had been learning and using encryption along with a powerful new decentralized virtual currency called Bitcoin. The online magazine had suggested that each recruit obtain a legal Bitcoin debit card, which could be used to pay for initial travel expenses to the Middle East.

Each of the 4 Australian born Jihadists was now in possession of new Bitcoin debit cards that that permitted instant receipt of anonymous Bitcoin funding from Islamic State affiliates located anywhere in the world.

Many shops and businesses across Australia had been early adopters of the technology. Along with many other tech savvy Australians his age, Abdul had been using Bitcoin for more than a year.

During his early usage, Abdul had read that the Australian Federal Counter Terrorism Police were carefully watching all local Bitcoin exchange transactions.

In order to avoid any future links with "Islamic funding", as labeled by the state-run media, Abdul had opened an account with a Bitcoin exchange located in New Zealand called Exchange-NZ.net.

This non-Australian online exchange did not require strict customer identification as required by the Australian government. In fact, on deposits and transactions of less than $2,000 AUD no identification was even required. There were also many other Internet accessible exchanges around the world that permitted Bitcoin transactions without strict ID requirements. When opening this account, Abdul, had just verified his email address, and that was all the identification needed to operate a new NZ trading account. The Exchange-NZ.net had even permitted local cash deposits, in Australian banks, by third parties.

This cash deposit procedure Abdul used for purchasing and selling Bitcoin had allowed him to avoided all local restrictive bank regulations. Each customer's buy order is quickly matched with another person's listed sell order. In such a transaction, the NZ company was not acting as a currency exchange, but merely matching buyers with sellers for private transactions. This high volume Bitcoin exchange had managed to avoid all of the usual bank restrictions, anti-money laundering regulations, and ID requirements.

27

However, the transaction fee for this service was almost three times the average exchange fees.

Month's earlier, when Abdul had placed a buy order for $2,000 AUD of Bitcoin, Exchange-NZ.com had matched his purchase order with sellers in that price range. While to completely fill his $2,000 AUD, Bitcoin buy order had taken three small partial orders, all of the transactions, had been completed in 1 business day.

Some successful Kiwi entrepreneur had created a Bitcoin market "workaround", which had allowed Abdul to engage in Bitcoin transactions as a resident of Australia without any worry of being tracked by the Australian authorities. The Bitcoin advice received from the Islamic State online magazine was proving very useful.

After a year of successful buying and selling on Exchange-NZ.net, Abdul and his three friends were now ready to undertake the journey from Australia to Syria and begin training.

Associates within the Islamic State had provided the Bitcoin funding for their mission.

An anonymous wallet address was made available by Abdul, which had received Bitcoins covering the total cost of each recruit's travel to the Middle East. Since the jihad recruits had legally obtained the debit cards, and the Bitcoin could not be traced, the new fighter's travel funding had quietly taken place without any issues.

Santa Clarita, California

Jan was a single mom living in Santa Clarita, California. She was a waitress by day and on most nights earned extra cash cleaning offices in the nearby hospital. She hated the grueling work. However, it had been a goal of Jan's to provide her son with a good education so that he could make something of himself.

Now 17 years old, her only son Andrew would be graduating from Golden Valley High School next year. She was supremely proud of him. Over the past 15 years, she had saved up $28,000 which all would go towards his first few years in a good college.

All her life, Jan had been a manic saver, cutting corners on food shopping, electric bills and even selling her car in favor of inexpensive bus rides. Throughout her life, it had been incredibly hard to save any money. Each time she went without lunch or sat patiently on a crowded bus, she envisioned her son graduating college from a large well known university. His diploma would make all of her struggle worth it.

For the past year, she had heard about a promising new method of payment called Bitcoin. There were many articles talking about the currency's growth potential, and how so many young people who invested early had retired. Jan was always on the lookout for high yielding investments. At the moment, her entire $28,000 fortune sat in a PayPal money market account.

One day while reading about local California utility stocks, Jan had received an email in her Hotmail box, and the subject line had mentioned Bitcoins. The email looked very official and offered a free subscription to an investment newsletter related to High Yielding Investment Programs. Jan clicked the email link requesting a newsletter and moments later her first issue arrived.

The colorful newsletter linked to a current issue of another investment newsletter called the Global Investment Web Street Journal. It was a familiar looking document, almost identical to a newsletter that her local credit union had published on investments.

The High Yielding Investment Trusts shown in the online material were all paying much more than PayPal's money market fund.

The newsletter also had information on the improving US economy, and again she saw even more information on the promising new Bitcoin virtual currency. Jan had read about how Bitcoin was the money of the future. She did not understand how the decentralized currency worked, but had connected the earlier articles about how many young investors were making millions in Bitcoin. All of the Investment Trusts listed in this newsletter accepted Bitcoin, in fact, that was the only method for transferring money to and from a trust.

Jan had wanted to become involved in Bitcoin, and the professional newsletter offered her several apparently legitimate high yield investment opportunities.

A company called Global Web Street Publishing had distributed the impressive financial document. The information clearly stated the publishing company had no association with the actual trusts. The front of the paper had a picture of an older gentleman, identified as Dr. Frederic Williams, an accredited investor, and Ph.D. She believed that this exciting newsletter would provide her with unbiased recommendations. Amazingly, the last page of the bulletin clearly stated that it was offering 100% independent, unbiased recommendations. Plus, the newsletter linked to an online forum where buyers discussed the Bitcoin "Trust Investments". She felt honored to have such inside information.

Jan quietly acknowledged that she did not understand all of the topics. However, the newsletter detailed the specifics of investing with Bitcoin and how to stay safe with at least six confirmations. It also directly linked to the website of the Bitcoin Business Foundation Center. She had previously heard of the Bitcoin Business Foundation Center and was pleased to see it listed in the material. Although, she did not see the newsletter or trust investments listed on the center's website. Jan figured that the center may be prohibited from publicly recording "investments". She also saw that this particular was being actively discussed on the forums.

Jan was blown away by the incredible high yields and excellent annual returns offered by the Bitcoin investments. She felt Bitcoin was the money of the future, and she wanted to participate. The 1.4% to 3.2% daily return seemed almost too-good-to-be-true. However, she had been following the HYIP investments for more than 3 weeks and the private Bitcoin Investment Trust, had been making all of the scheduled regular payments.

Reading about all those Bitcoin millionaires and how they had made so much money in digital currency, Bitcoin seemed to be the way that young, smart people made money in today's world. Jan truly felt that she could now be a part of this Bitcoin success.

One of the Trust Programs, she was following each day called the "Assured Investment Plan" had looked particularly attractive. It was paying interest of 1.4% daily for a period of 190 days, at which time investors had the option to roll over the initial investment for another 190 days or withdraw the funds. She had watched the payouts for almost a month and felt the investment was right on track.

The financial gurus operating for the Trust were reported to be trading in and out of digital currency for enormous profits and sharing that money with their investors. They would use the investor's money for trading and as compensation for the utilization of these funds; the Trust would pay a small portion of the earnings back to investors. She had heard of something like that before on Wall Street, and Jan thought it was called a mutual fund.

She calculated that it should take a $20,000 investment from her PayPal account to put her over-the-top on her son's college education fund. A $20,000 investment would grow to more than $50,000 by the end of her 190 days. She then recognized that $50,000 was a lot more than her current $28,000 in savings currently earning next to nothing in the PayPal money market account. With $50,000, she could secure several years of her son's future in a good college and even help with his rent.

She was now excited to be making a Bitcoin investment. However, Jan would first need to learn how to exchange her dollars into Bitcoin.

Burbank, California

A Bitcoin enthusiast and early adopter, Raj had first studied the new cryptocurrency alongside his father in 2011. There had been many discussions around the dinner table, whether Satoshi Nakamoto was a real person or a group of private mathematicians who had collectively used a pseudonym.

After reading Nakamoto's white paper, Raj wanted to believe that one person had been responsible for creating the virtual currency. However, as the months grew into years and Bitcoin had become more of a commercial product, his father had convinced him that

Bitcoin's "single person theory" was flawed. The family's conclusion was that a group of government hired cypherpunks had collectively designed Bitcoin. It may have even been possible that the group was working for a government funded entity such as the Defense Advanced Research Projects Agency (DARPA). After all, so many federal regulatory agencies had given Bitcoin the "green light" over the past few years that the new "government cypherpunk" theory had seemed appropriate.

For more than a decade, his father had maintained a vice president position at a well-known aerospace company. Raj's mom took care of the home and volunteered at a local food bank several times a week. Both parents were big supporters of the California Republican Party and Raj had followed in their footsteps.

An only child, he had been born in California a year after his parents had emigrated from India. They had filled their house with high-tech gadgets, including the newest computers, smartphones, and ultra-high definition TVs. All of the family's electronic devices were wired into the home's blazing fast Internet connection. With computers positioned next to their dinner plates, each night both he and his father worked their laptops during supper.

Now in his second year of college, Raj had become a summer intern for the California Republican Party. Working in their Burbank office all summer, he was planning to remain in the program until the start of fall classes. His parents had graciously arranged the internship and Raj was pleased to have such an influential summer job.

Raqqa, Syria

The Islamic banks throughout the region had created a roadblock to Amir's proposed widespread use of Bitcoin funding in the Islamic State. The local people and businesses had been reluctant to use Bitcoin, because, no Islamic bank would accept a Bitcoin business. Except for several significant agents in Dubai, there were very few exchange points in the region.

In a currency exchange business, Arabs require face-to-face locations. For the players throughout a region to engage in a daily digital currency business, there needed to be many shop locations for the face-to-face exchange of Bitcoin into local Dirham paper currency.

Employees of Islamic banks were being told to consider Bitcoin as haram, and it was proving impossible for Islamic banks to accept or even understand Bitcoin transactions. Many Arab businessmen in the region also incorrectly believed that Bitcoin payments could be easily traced by the American government.

Attempting to correct these rumors, Amir had written a short, educational paper detailing the advantages of the Bitcoin platform, entitled "Advancing Charitable Islamic Donations in Bitcoin." Throughout the mainstream press and across the Muslim world, many famous people had been widely quoting this work.

Just a few years earlier, Amir had seen houses filled with cash in tiny Afghan villages, where the Taliban leaders would bring raw opium and instantly exchange it for stacks of Afghanis. However, none of those dealers would have ever taken part in the exchange of Bitcoin virtual currency.

Syria, however, was much different. Amir had quietly approached the hawala networks and requested they handle his local Bitcoin-cash exchanges. The hawaladars were already responsible for a majority of payments inside the systems of the Islamic State, including monthly payments to fighters.

More than a year ago, Amir had directed his trusted agent to seek out and find local Syrian and Iraqi hawalandars that could exchange Bitcoins for cash. Almost immediately, his agent had reported the connection with a very well-respected hawaladar in Syria who operated as part an extensive regional hawala network.

The routine had included Bitcoin being locally accepted by the hawala network in exchange for cash. Amir had been executing a face-to-face Bitcoin transfer using his smartphone's mobile Bitcoin wallet and then receiving money. The hawalander would then sell the Bitcoin though a group of Dubai finance & trading companies that also engaged in currency exchange. The companies were run by two Iranian brothers. There was no way to link the Bitcoin payments with the Islamic State and because of the hawaladar's 50 years of operation in the region, the brothers would never question him.

This regional hawala network, which operated from Syria, was one of the largest and wealthiest channels currently being used by Arab businessmen to transfer money and finance global jihad campaigns. It was a powerful reciprocal arrangement known as the "iron triangle" closely linking the hawala dealers in the region with Afghan heroin kingpins and Islamic militants.

Over the past year, Amr's new arrangement with the hawala network had been operating very well. The Bitcoin exchanges and transfers had created a seamless cross-border route for direct anonymous donations to the Islamic State. Those Persian businessmen, who had been so worried about wire transfers claimed, "One cannot send a bank transfer to a mujahidin without Western governments becoming immediately aware of the funding source." However, now they could use Bitcoin and anonymously support the Islamic State.

Denver, Colorado

The four new electronic marijuana vending machines had safely arrived at Mr. Green's locations around Denver. Store managers had placed each unit inside a shop, and they were now plugged in and functioning. No one under 21 was allowed to enter the buildings. This restriction screened customers by age, permitting anyone inside the locations to use the machine without producing and ID.

Georgina, along with all of the store managers, were new to Bitcoin. They all needed the vending machine company representative to walk them through the machine's operation and the customers' transaction process. As Georgina and her managers stood quietly next to one of the new machines, the company rep loaded small packages of various buds and edibles into the freezer sized metal cabinet.

These climate-controlled, vending machines offered fresh marijuana in vacuum packed, sealed plastic bags, including edibles such as chocolates and baked goods. These new machines delivered a variety of benefits for Mr. Green's customers. An automated checkout process was much faster than talking to a salesman at the counter. Automated machines saved money because it did not require any paid full-time staff. Employees could also more easily track store inventory that cut down on employee theft. Also, Georgina found that customers who were reluctant to approach the large sales counter and talk with an employee, could discretely buy from the machine and quietly exit with their package.

Completing a vending machine sale with Bitcoin, is very similar to a supermarket automatic self-checkout line. The machine totals up a customer's order, and a QR code is available for payment. The customer would scan the QR code with a mobile device, pay the requested amount in Bitcoin.

After payment, the products would be distributed through a compartment door on the front of the machine. This Bitcoin virtual currency payment process was identical to paying for any other Bitcoin retail goods in Colorado.

The two mystery issues for Georgina were generating & paying sales tax on each Bitcoin transaction and also converting the Bitcoin into dollars before the market price had a chance to move lower.

Since Mr. Green's had no bank account, an IRS tax agent in the Denver office had recommended creating an unrelated holding company through another state such as Delaware. Accountants could then link this new corporation with Mr. Green's by something as simple as a DBA filing. The third party corporate entity could then electronically process tax payments on behalf of Mr. Green's. This process would stop the company from being fined and keep it up to date for all tax payments.

With no other options available, Georgina reluctantly followed this advice and created a Delaware company named Green Bitcoin Trading Corporation. The somewhat elaborate corporate set up had been designed, at the suggestion of a Federal Government Employee, for the purpose of maintaining a bank account and electronically paying quarterly government taxes on time.

After reviewing the corporate structure with her local accountant, Georgina took the operation one step further. The out of state bank account she had opened for the new shell company allowed for the regular exchange Mr. Green's Bitcoins into bankable dollars. She had found a company called BitStarter.com, operating out of San Francisco that Green Bitcoin Trading could use as a new Bitcoin exchange and bank.

The store's BitStarter.com account now processed millions of Bitcoin and US dollars were being returned to her new shell corporation bank account. All taxes were now being paid on time, and the operation was working just as the IRS employee had recommended. Georgina thought to herself, "For once those idiots collaborated with me to produce an agreeable bank workaround. Thank you, Mr. Taxman."

In the application for corporate services, Georgina had designated the Green Bitcoin Trading Corporation in Delaware as a virtual currency trading and currency exchange business. She did not disclose any link to the marijuana business.

For Mr. Green's Dispensary, the new daily exchange of Bitcoin had become an inexpensive and simple operation.

Location Unknown

Bota was a world-class hacker and Bitcoin freak. At just 19, he was operating a modern Bitcoin laundry service through the most popular Darknet drug bazaar called Red-Path.

Between the market sellers, Bota's laundry service, was the most popular tumbler on the website. More than 300,000 dollars in Bitcoins had been circulated each day through his laundry wallets.

Also known as a mixer or a tumbler, Bota's Bitcoin laundry service would take an amount of Bitcoins from an unknown party, bounce and scramble them through multiple wallets and various transactions. Once mixed or tumbled to disguise its past, Bota would the then pay the Bitcoins back to the client, minus his fee. The "clean" Bitcoins could arrive with the customer in one amount, or many smaller transactions spread out over a period. For the very private clients, he suggested a workable personalized strategy with each customer. Bota could tell a lot about the origin and source of a client's funds from the way they communicated with him.

In basic terms, his laundry service disguised the origin of the funds within the Bitcoin blockchain. Bota often used a metaphor to help explain his business. He would say, "Picture, a giant school of fish swimming through the ocean, you could catch a few fish, throw them back into the ocean and be guaranteed that the next fish caught from that school would not be the same ones."

The laundry's fee on each cleaned transaction included a percentage on the total amount of Bitcoins cleaned, plus a small fee on each outgoing transaction.

Bota had worked for several years servicing only private clients. He moved tens of millions of dollars in Bitcoin through his laundry, never knowing where any of the coins had come from until Mt. Gox closed. Matching the contiguous large flow of Bitcoin stolen from Mt. Gox accounts, with the amounts and timing of his private laundry cycles, Bota concluded that his employers had been the ones doing the stealing. "Good for them," he thought.

The admin of the old Silkroad has prominently listed his laundry on that website. However, today was something of a new day in the world of online Bitcoin drug sales. Today, more drugs were sold online, and more laundry-tumblers were in use on the Darknet than ever before.

A concerned group of parents known as the Digital-Citizens-Something-or-Other, recently published a report showing that today there were more active Red-Path drug seller listings than had been ever previously available on Silkroad. The report claimed that Red-Path had something like 14,000 drug listing with more than 40,000 products and that low number did not include any other online Darknet markets. Coincidentally, many of those sellers were using Bota's laundry!

God bless Bitcoin; he thought to himself.

Part 2

<u>Portland, Oregon</u>

> Because of the ease at which digital currency can circulate over the Internet, it has become the favorite tool of many transnational criminal organizations. Any Bitcoin investigation that begins in one US city will almost certainly cross both state and federal jurisdictional boundaries.
> ~Unnamed Drug Enforcement Administration Agent, Baltimore, Maryland

The four bedroom house was located in the Portland suburbs, about a 12-minute drive from downtown. There were no bus lines in that area and no one ever visited the house, except the four people that lived there.

Joaquin ran the entire operation. He and his girlfriend Lucia had rented the middle-class property about a year ago. The whole time the couple had been living there in the suburbs selling Methamphetamine. Lucia and Joaquin were both Mexican nationals, but Joaquin had a legal Oregon driver's license and a local yard work business. His white Ford F150 with a wire trailer on the back, hauled his mowers, leaf blowers, and rakes. He figured this was the perfect cover, driving around town pulling the mower and equipment cutting grass. He could pick up kilos of meth in Vancouver and bring them back into Portland. No one, not even the neighbors, suspected the Mexican yardman of selling drugs for the cartels. He even paid his rent with money orders bought from a nearby gas station and Lucia told the realtor that Joaquin got paid each week in cash for his lawn work.

The meth business brought in bushels of cash, and almost all of it went back to Mexico through Vancouver. That was not his side of the enterprise. Joaquin stored his cash under the house, in a homemade poured concrete box. Having no US bank account, he moved most of his personal wealth through Bitcoin. The bulk of his profits were transferred directly back to his family in Juarez, Mexico.

For those without a US bank account, such as Joaquin, Bitcoin was the ultimate financial tool. Workers in the United States were able to bounce Bitcoin money it right over the border, avoiding the expensive old money service businesses that raped customers with high fees. Bitcoin was slowly giving his business and "his people", great power over the banks. He had transferred more than a million US dollars in Bitcoin back to Mexico many times and never even had to show his ID.

There were even Bitcoin ATMs now operating in both Juarez and Tijuana. Bitcoin was giving Latinos an advantage in the financial world. He hoped that a significant exchange would soon open which could serve Mexico and Latin America. Joaquin laughed as he said aloud, "Banks? We don't need no stinking banks!"

Bitcoin was changing his world for the better. There had been a slogan going around town, it was, "The world runs on Bitcoin," and now he understood what that meant. Bitcoin fueled his sales and was the primary tool that facilitated significant financial transactions in his illegal world.

He was a mid-level dealer, buying a kilo or two each week and selling large parcels online through Red-path and other darknet sites. His computer set up was useful, but not impressive. He used two laptops they had purchased from Walmart and a few prepaid cell phones, also from Walmart.

The two younger girls living there with him and Lucia were skilled small time couriers. Both girls had clean backgrounds without any arrests. That also meant their prints were not on file with any law enforcement agency.

Several times a week, the girls went into Portland, dropping off the outgoing packages and selling the Bitcoins for cash. Post offices, UPS mailing centers and even private mailbox operations of the larger apartment buildings all could accept the ordinary looking parcels. In reality, they were sending meth all over the United States. First-class mail and priority included tracking and were very inexpensive to use. In over a year, they had never lost a package.

The underground darknet websites and forums were ideal places to market meth. He sold ounces and sometimes pounds, never small amounts. Business was booming. Since the online drug bazaars and forums had opened a few years earlier, it was like shooting fish in a barrel, sale after sale, Bitcoins coming in like mad. Because there were no face-to-face sales, there was no chance of being arrested handing off a package.

Accessible only through the Tor network, the many online bazaars with names like The Black Market, Red-Path, and The Pirate's Trading Cove were all doing a booming Bitcoin business. Methamphetamine was their drug of choice. He had even purchased a dozen fake state drivers licenses for his two couriers, just in case the cops grabbed them up. With fake IDs, they could walk out on bond and disappear, and then nothing would lead back to him.

All of the meth sales took place online. While the mountain of Bitcoins flowed into his wallets, the girls mailed packages every few days. During the week, he mowed a few lawns, raked leaves in the fall and acted like the "Mexican Yardman".

God Bless America, he thought to himself.

It was just about 3:00 in the afternoon and Joaquin sat at the dinner table finishing a bottle of red wine.

Dirty dishes and leftover enchilada casserole sat on the table in front of him alongside his two laptops. Each was open and connected through the house's WI-Fi into the Tor browser. He was online with his Red-path seller pages and two of his other darknet seller websites. The orders and the Bitcoins just came flowing in, more and more each week.

One of the girls had just finished wrapping today's final delivery box, which she had stuffed with an ounce of high-quality Mexican meth. Clarisa was always careful to package the boxes using plenty of tape, "no chance these were coming open by accident", she thought.

Next to her was a pile of small wrapped boxes she would later mail. Each parcel looked very similar, showing USPS Priority Mail labels.

She was shipping a total of 17 ounces that afternoon; it had been a busy and profitable few days.

Once finished with the final box, she carefully packed all of them into her reusable New Seasons cloth grocery bag and set it just inside the front door.

Her sidekick, Jenny, was leaving for the Tuesday Bitcoin Meetup and would be providing her a ride into town. She knew, the Bitcoin Meetups were the most boring game in town, but those geeks always had the big cash. The weekly Meetup was a great place to buy or sell Bitcoins.

As they exited the house, she grabbed her overstuffed canvas bag and computer. The Apple laptop proudly displayed a large QR code sticker on the lid. The QR code represented her anonymous Bitcoin payment and trading account. Buyers would scan the QR code and transfer funds. It bore no name or personal identifying items; it was just a code that in reality concealed yet another code, which was the wallet file. Jenny was able to sell 20-35,000 dollars in Bitcoin at each meeting, often carrying out a pocketbook full of cash. The Meetups were all about cash buyers, some of the usual locals traded Bitcoin every day for profit and they brought lots of cash.

As they climbed into the blue Nissan Versa, Jenny slipped her laptop under the driver's seat and took the wheel while Clarisa placed her cloth bag onto the back seat and softly closed the passenger door. They were off to downtown Portland engaging in criminal activity, just as they did just about each weekday.

Raqqa, Syria

For the past year and a half, Amir had been responsible for media recruitment through affiliates in Africa, Canada, and the United States. His new full color digital online magazine had become a powerful recruiting tool and a jewel in the Islamic State's media crown. Through the digital magazine, he had advised all recruits to obtain Bitcoin debit cards.

This bank issued card gave Syrian recruiters the ability to fund new fighters directly in foreign countries, including the United States.

Bitcoin was the source and method of this funding. Amir was able to send Bitcoins instantly and pay for the new fighter's travel from their home country to the Middle East.

As an unknown third party, militants in Syria had been able to send Bitcoins anonymously to these debit cards and silently fund all travel expenses for new recruits from Africa and the United States. Several recruits leaving from Michigan had paid for plane tickets and hotels with the Bitcoin plastic that had been funded directly by the Islamic State. These new fighters were not yet on any country's "watch list" and they had no problem obtaining an inexpensive card from the issuing Singapore Bitcoin exchange.

Anyone's Bitcoin wallet could be used to load money onto these cards, thus hiding the original owner and the source of the funds. Issued by a legitimate financial company in Singapore, the plastic, even permitted cash withdrawals from Western ATMs. Through this anonymous money transfer, Bitcoin debit cards had become a very effective financing tool for the Jihad network.

Amir had proven that third party Bitcoin funding could be used to purchase airline tickets, rent vehicles, withdraw cash from ATMs and pay for hotels. All of the new recruits, guided by Amir, had been able to obtain cards easily while living in their home country. Today, two more recruits were being funded thus beginning their journey to Syria and Amir was happy to pay their way.

Seattle, Washington

Julia and Steven felt blessed to have created such a rewarding and profitable Bitcoin mining business. Each month, they saved 3 Bitcoins from their newly mined currency and donated them to three charities identified and supported by the Bitcoin community.

Their first non-profit this month to receive one Bitcoin was the California Republican Party. The California GOP was the first of all the West Coast political party offices to accept Bitcoin. The Bitcoin community was supporting the party, and the couple was also interested in providing Bitcoin support. Neither a Democrat nor

Republican, Steven directly supported the party that backed Bitcoin. In this case, it was the Republicans.

Bitcoin had made Julia feel connected to a powerful global network community. Because one person can directly transfer Bitcoin to every other Bitcoin wallet on earth, she now envisioned the entire world as her local Bitcoin neighborhood.

Her next charity donation was a perfect example of Bitcoin's global reach. A group aiding those injured and left homeless in Ukraine had held up a Bitcoin QR code requesting donations during a BBC newscast. Julia had been resourceful enough to grab her phone and scan that QR code from the TV screen. Both she and Steven had decided this brave group helping others in Ukraine should receive the second Bitcoin donation this month. They did not know the group's name or website, but the broadcast had talked about the how many helpful things the group was doing for the injured, and they wanted to help.

It only took a second for the Bitcoin to travel all the way from Seattle to Ukraine. Both Julia and Steven marveled at how they were helping to change the world using Bitcoin.

Before his involvement with Bitcoin, Steven had never donated any money to charities and frankly, he had never even thought about making charitable donations. However, today he and Julia considered themselves an integral part of Bitcoin's charitable community.

This month was unusual for Steven, today marked the sixth month in a row, and they had donated Bitcoins to The Africa Clean Water team (ACW). Their donations had helped to drill water wells and provide training to local villages for the continued operation of new clean drinking water wells. "If you teach a man to fish...." Julia thought to herself.

Last month, Steven had received a file of hi-res photos showing the new water wells, along with the images of children drinking the clean water. The Bitcoin community had been responsible for those healthy smiles.

Steven had boldly marked the GPS map coordinates of every newly drilled well, on a wall map of West Africa which now hung near their kitchen table.

Similar to Steven, Julia had never before been a part of charitable donations. The Bitcoin community had convinced her to give some Bitcoins back to those in need. She made sure that each month they supported the charities that accepted Bitcoin.

West Africa

James headed up the Africa Clean Water team (ACW), a non-profit that had drilled more than 14 brand new wells in the past 24 months. Those wells were now providing clean drinking water to villages and rural areas of Nigeria. The entire charity water program had only been possible because of a new Internet currency called Bitcoin.

In Africa, there were many clean water non-profit groups working to supply fresh drinking water. However, ACW was the only organization that had received its entire funding through virtual currency donations. The Bitcoins had been continuously flowing in each week for the past two years.

Never had the non-profit world seen a global community of like-minded people contributing so generously to clean drinking water. Members of the Bitcoin community regularly engaged the ACW team through encouraging emails, Skype calls and mailing clothing and medicine. The Bitcoin community of young users had followed through on a big promise of clean drinking water for Nigerian communities in need.

The entire ACW team was enthusiastic about leveraging the Bitcoin technology to help improve the non-profit world.

James ran the charity organization, and his headquarters were in the capital city of Lagos, Nigeria. He understood the dire need for clean water across Africa and how ACW's new wells were making a difference. Early in the program, the group had encountered dozens of villages that lacked any clean water. The dirty water regularly caused sickness and even death. While scouting locations for new wells, their team had encountered several young children whose faces had been partially eaten by bacteria from waterborne diseases. It had been heartbreaking to witness such misery.

Burbank, California

During his first week, and every week since, Raj had made sure that everyone in the California Republican Party office knew that he was a Bitcoin enthusiast and early adopter.

Every member of his family was a Bitcoin fanatic. Both parents used the virtual currency for online shopping. Bitcoin was even used to send global money transfers back to relatives in India, and it had become his father's preferred online method of payment. Raj even had a Bitcoin debit card, which his mother sometimes used to send him college money without his father's knowledge!

Early in the year, the independent regulatory agency that administers and enforces federal campaign finance laws, known as the Federal Election Commission (FEC), had issued an Advisory Opinion that paved the way for Bitcoin to be legally accepted as a political donation.

For Republican candidates, this was big news because the FEC had jurisdiction over campaign financing for the U.S. House of Representatives, the U.S. Senate, the Presidency and the Vice Presidency.

Raj imagined that one day soon he would be able to send Bitcoin donations in support of the next Republican candidate for President and the family hoped that would be Bobby Jindal. The FEC also concluded that political campaigns may use funds from a campaign depository to purchase Bitcoins for investment purposes, provided the Bitcoin funds are returned to the treasury before they are used to make disbursements.

While this news had gone mostly unnoticed in Washington political circles, Republican candidates at the state level were now actively engaging in Bitcoin discussions.

Raj immediately began working on a Bitcoin mobile app for Republican donations and an HTML campaign contribution template for his Republican candidate friends. It was rare that any registered voter would use a credit card to make a donation with a smartphone. Mobile users only donated about 1% of all of the year's previous contributions.

However, because of the convenience of using a cell phone for Bitcoin payments, most users were already sending and receiving payments through a mobile wallet. There were several famous Bitcoin mobile wallets and even SMS platforms that facilitated the transfer of Bitcoins for non-smartphone mobile users.

During the past 24 months, the convenience, of using Bitcoin mobile payments, had already been well established. Raj felt that Bitcoin GOP campaign donations from mobile devices would eventually become commonplace.

He had even drafted a sample voice message script for Bitcoin campaign donations. It reads:

"Welcome to the future, as you may have heard our campaign/office now accepts Bitcoin. Virtual Currency is a safe and secure method of payment. If you are a US citizen and would like to contribute Bitcoin to this campaign, please visit our website at [candidate's domain URL] and click on the "Bitcoin Accepted Here" button. Every Bitcoin donated is used to spread a message of bold, conservative, reform and support Republican candidates throughout the great State of California."

Information included in all Bitcoin donation website templates would also contain the following disclosure.

"Hello voters! California law permits political campaigns to accept contributions of currency or other assets such as Bitcoin. Because the state and federal laws do not currently recognize Bitcoin as a currency, all Bitcoin contributions to Republican candidates will be listed as an in-kind contribution. In determining the monetary value of a Bitcoin contribution, the campaign office would use the current market value of Bitcoin at the time of the transaction."

That afternoon, after Raj had added the Bitcoin donation button on the California Republican Party website, every major TV station in California had reported on the story. This story had legs!

The party's BitStarter.com donation account quickly began filling up with Bitcoins. On Friday, just three days later, Raj calculated that the number of contributors in the US totaled more than 2,800 people.

Adding Bitcoin to the GOP platform in California had been a stroke of genius, and Raj had received all the credit.

Since donations had all come from individuals and not corporations, the office was buzzing to find out just who had been donating using Bitcoin.

Denver, Colorado

With total sales of Colorado recreational marijuana surging to more than 6 million dollars a week, Bitcoin was quickly becoming a possible popular option for players in the new Marijuana industry.

Mr. Green's Dispensary had been receiving Bitcoins, transferring ownership of them to a third party shell company and selling them each day through BitStarter.com. Georgina watched as BitStarter.com automatically deposited the sales proceeds back to the associated Delaware business account.

In reality, the new financial setup was a complicated bank workaround for a problem entirely created by the federal government's antiquated war on drugs.

Georgina thought to herself, "If the banks were permitted to work directly with Colorado's legal marijuana sellers, we would not have to engage in a corporate shell game. If Mr. Green's could have a bank account, there would be no headaches."

After three weeks, the new Bitcoin sales and exchange system was working extremely well. Every banking day, the BitStarter.com account had seamlessly converted all of Mr. Green's incoming Bitcoins into dollars, which appeared nightly in the Delaware bank.

The bank workaround had been operating for everyone's benefit. More and more, new customers were lined up paying with Bitcoin through the easy-to-use electronic vending machines.

Georgina was impressed and ordered six more machines. Additionally, all of the salespeople begin accepting Bitcoin over-the-counter in all store locations. She even installed 5 Bitcoin ATMs in all of the locations. This move enabled Mr. Green's to make additional profit selling Bitcoins back to incoming customers who then used them to purchase retail goods through her stores.

Location Unknown

Bota and two friends had been attempting to hack their way into a Bitcoin wallet service provider in Poland. They were exploiting a vulnerability and hacking a Linode cloud service. The target company kept "secure" hot wallets on the server, and it was Bota's job to compromise the customer service portal then gain access to the wallets through the cloud server.

The attack was accomplished by compromising a chain of email accounts which eventually allowed Bota, and one of his associates, to reset the password for the Linode server and thus gain access using a newly created password.

A server had to be rented in Poland so that it wouldn't raise any IP location red flags for the email recovery. Tracking IP addresses and geolocation was a security mechanism. However, it could also become the perfect cover to disguise a hacker's location during entry.

Six weeks into the job, the team had accessed the Linode server. Bota cleared out more than 34,000 Bitcoin in this action. The company, which ran the online wallet service, immediately went out of business, and the hack caused Bitcoin losses for all of their clients.

Bota thought to himself, "Too bad for them, holding Bitcoins in a hot wallet on a virtual cloud server is the equivalent of leaving a stack of cash sitting on the server. It was my cash now."

He transferred the Bitcoins into his laundry accounts and began the process of cleaning them before he would liquidate the shiny new coins.

Beverly Hills, California

Even by Beverly Hills standards, the offices of Allen, Smith and Cohen, professional accountants, and financial services were lavish. Todd entered the conference room where Larry had been waiting and began to speak.

"Good morning Lawrence, how are you today?" said Todd. Larry quickly corrects him, "Todd, please call me Larry." Todd responds, "Excellent."

As they both sit, Todd leaned in towards Larry and began speaking in a soft tone. "Mr. Levine has explained to me that you are looking to acquire a large amount of Bitcoins for long term investment."

"Yes, that is correct. I have a number US bank accounts with large balances, which I'd now like to move discretely into Bitcoin out of sight, for a long term hold," replied Larry.

Todd, "We can do this for you as we have for several other of Mr. Levine's private clients. We also provide the security of cold storage for all long-term investments."

Larry asks, "What is cold storage?"

Todd replies, "Well, Bitcoins are not like other assets such as gold, diamonds or real estate. Bitcoin is virtual; it's a digital file that you, as the owner, would keep in a digital wallet. Think of it as a bearer certificate, whoever owns the file, gets the money. It's not always safe to keep this file online or on a computer drive. If someone hacks the computer, the file can be stolen. If the hardware fails, the Bitcoin can be lost forever. In either of those cases, you will lose 100% of your invested funds."

Larry responds, "I don't like the sound of that...."

Todd says, "Neither do we. That's why when you work with us, we remove the file from the digital wallet, print out a paper wallet, and store it here offline in our secure vault. This process is called cold storage. Again, please think of this as a bearer note, it won't have your name or social security number on it or any legal way to link the ownership of those funds to you. Bitcoin is a cash type asset."

Larry tells him, "Ok."

Todd continues on explaining the investment procedure, "Anytime you wish to turn those Bitcoin back into cash, you simply stop by our offices and we will remove the printed document from our vault and turn it back into cash for you. It can be wired anywhere in the world, as you request, and you may cash out the entire amount or even just portions."

"What about the paper trail from my bank to the Bitcoins?" asked Larry.

Todd responds, "That's not a problem, we are a licensed California financial and accounting firm. We often move and transfer vast sums of money on behalf of our private Beverly Hills clientele. To begin your purchase of Bitcoin, you simply wire into our primary funds account here at the firm and we back you up with the necessary tax paperwork anytime in the future should you request it. How much of an investment are you looking to store in Bitcoin?"

Larry asks, "What is the necessary paperwork?"

Todd responds, "We work with several overseas lending agents and leasing companies. If we need to show that the funds are legally residing in a jurisdiction overseas, this is no problem."

Larry continues asking questions, "Where overseas?"

Todd now seemingly agitated tells him, "These are foreign jurisdictions that do not respond to court requests for asset discovery. They are companies that when asked, will not respond, other than to confirm the investment agreement with our California law firm and support our paperwork on behalf of clients."

Larry asked, "Her lawyers are going to see the recent withdrawals. Will it be legally possible to trace where they went? Can we back that up with paperwork to make it all legal?"

Todd calmly responds, "Another point we handle... Even though, we are dealing with overseas operations, our clients are not required to file FBAR tax forms. Larry, we are professionals, we know what we are doing."

Now Todd leaned back in his chair, looked out the window and said to him, "Larry perhaps this type of "investment" is not for you."

Quickly, Larry speaks up, "Well, I'm thinking about 12 million dollars or more." Todd smiles and now nods his head in the affirmative, "Superb."

Larry responds, "Is 15 million a problem or a bit higher?"

Todd, "No problem at all, just give us an approximate time frame for the incoming funds, and we will arrange the Bitcoin for you."

Larry asks, "What is your firm's fee?"

Todd, "We charge a 5% fee to purchase the Bitcoin and a 2% on the exit sales." Larry replies, "That seems steep."

Todd, "Larry, in this world you get what you pay for, and we have been supporting our clients' Bitcoin investments and backing them up with paperwork for almost two years. There has never been an issue. When you work with our firm, Larry, you are working with the best. Your money goes down the digital rabbit hole and can never be linked to you until you ask us to retrieve it. From that point, it's just 24 hours getting back into your bank accounts. Bitcoin is even better than a Swiss bank account. Plus, you can avoid the long flight to Geneva."

Larry, "How many days does it require to close the transaction and accept ownership of the Bitcoin?"

Todd, "Bitcoins are a digital version of cash, all transactions, buys or sells, clear within minutes and cannot be reversed. No waiting, the moment your wired funds clear our account, you own the Bitcoin moments later."

Larry, "Can the IRS or the bank snoops find these Bitcoin and legally connect them to me?"

Todd, "Never. If you are under oath, you can truthfully say the funds don't exist and are not owned by you. When Bitcoins are held offline, in cold storage, the legal owner of them is the person in possession of the physical version of the digital file. Under California law, the person in possession of the record is the legal bearer and the owner of the funds. We will be holding the file in cold storage, we will be in physical possession of the Bitcoin and legally you do not own them. Our clients routinely make statements or declarations of this type under oath, and it is the truth. If you kept the Bitcoins on a paper wallet in your pocket or your home safe, technically you are in possession and would have to disclose your ownership to the court during the divorce."

Larry asks, "How about 17 million, is that a problem for your company?"

Todd answers, "Not a problem. We have methods to buy and sell large amounts of Bitcoin over the counter from large private sellers without affecting the market price."

Larry again questions, "Is there any price movement risk to my investment in Bitcoin? Does it go up and down in value like gold?"

Todd, "Yes, the value moves up and down each day just like a NASDAQ stock. However, our firm guarantees the amount you put into Bitcoin, will be the exact amount returned to you, minus our fee, of course. We take the price risk out of the equation so there is zero investment risk for you."

Larry finished the conversation with, "That sound splendid, and Bernie recommended you. Count on my transaction of 17 million dollars coming from about nine accounts. I can begin the transfers tomorrow."

Larry now pauses and extends his hand to shake in confirmation of the deal; he says, "If Bernie recommended you, I'm in."

Denver, Colorado

The bombshell hit exactly 30 days after Mr. Green's Dispensary began accepting Bitcoins. The incoming Bitcoin included both the counter sales along with the newer marijuana vending machines. That morning, Georgina received an email from BitStarter.com, regarding her new Delaware Bitcoin exchange and trading company.

> Dear Georgina Ray,
>
> We regret to inform you that Account number, XXXX-xXXX for Delaware Corporation XXX will be closed at the end of business on September 19th, two business days from today. Our company is prohibited by federal law from processing Bitcoin financial transactions for marijuana sales.
>
> At the time your firm's account was opened, it was not disclosed to BitStarter.com that the company's source of income was from the sale of legal marijuana in the State of Colorado. Failure to disclose this material fact is a violation of our terms of service. While you are engaged in a legal business under Colorado State Law, Federal law prohibits our company from transacting any Bitcoin payment processing for the sale of marijuana. This business is a practice that is still prohibited by federal law.
>
> At this time, the Bitcoin industry is very fragile. While your company has been our largest trading account, the discovery by our compliance department of involvement in the marijuana business creates an unsuitable risk for our business profile.
>
> All dollar denominated funds in the account, and all remaining Bitcoins will be immediately returned at the end of business today. Do not attempt to engage in any further trading in the account.

Unfortunately, the fractured regulatory structure of the United States creates an often complicated web of both federal and state laws. We appreciate your understanding in this matter. If the government decides to change the federal statutes in the future, we will be happy to reinstate your business account.

Thank you for your understanding.

Compliance Department

A hand delivered hard copy of this correspondence will arrive at your Denver headquarters within 24 hours.

This development was a new roadblock in Mr. Green's Bitcoin acceptance that could put the company out of business in a matter of days. Almost $1.7 million dollars a week in Bitcoin sales were being accepted through the enterprise's locations. While some of those coins were sold back to customers through the new ATMs, in order to keep the doors open, those remaining Bitcoin had to be exchanged for dollars on a daily basis. Despite the elaborate attempts at a bank workaround, Georgina was now stuck between a rock and a hard place.

Burgas, Bulgaria

Georgi's apartment was located on the building's eighth floor, and provided a beautiful western view of the bay. It was a very expensive setup, but these days, he was easily able to afford the rent. Georgi even permitted his two "computer helpers" to stay in the extra bedrooms while they worked for him.

The apartment's IT set up was top notch. There were five laptops, five desktop PCs and seven brand new smartphones, all of which were spread out on large wooden tables in the apartment's living room area. That summer on the Black Sea coast had been unusually hot and humid. Thankfully, Georgi's modern apartment was temperature controlled, and even with ten computers running full time, inside it had been very cool.

The smartphones provided bank access. Thanks to Bitcoin, they were able to move funds easily in and out of both Bulgarian Lev and EURO accounts. Georgi and his two helpers had been working as online support administrators and "hackers" for the well-known organization of businessmen known as the BLR-Group. Late last year, the FBI had labeled BLR a transnational criminal organization. For the past 23 months, he had been receiving his weekly funds from Moscow denominated in Bitcoin. During those last two years, Georgi and his helpers had maintained the BLR online forums and helped to hack over 3,000 US financial websites for BLR.

It was no accident that one of the world's largest Bitcoin exchanges, BGAexchange.bg, had their company headquarters nearby. This exchange business had been providing convenient direct Bitcoin banking services for many "businessmen" such as himself and his organization since it had opened in 2011. The BLR-Group was paying Georgi very well, and the top management had treated him with the respect he deserved.

While he had never met any of the other BLR hackers face-to-face, many in that group were operating from the city of Sofia, less than 400 kilometers away.

For the past eight years, Georgi had loved his work, hacking and cracking US computer systems. He remembered, from childhood how his family had given up Communism in the hope that his country would improve. Later, Bulgaria had joined the EU, in 2007, and the US had promised them improved living conditions. The business climate in his country did not improve. Today, for many poor Bulgarian people, conditions were much worse.

At 30 years old, he felt let down by the United States. His profitable revenge had been hacking into the financial systems of US businesses. In reality, each time he stole card and bank information the US was making his life better. He felt his career was working out well.

Georgi received his introduction to hacking in 2005 from one of his Mutra friends who now worked for the Bulgarian government.

Since he began hacking, Georgi knew that it was very difficult for the local Bulgarian Police to arrest hackers, and next to impossible for them to convict a local "businessmen" for hacking. Georgi and his friends operating in Sofia, Burgas and Varna had no problems with the police or government officials.

Lately, Georgi had been supplying his Russian BLR partners with massive amounts of stolen credit card data, and he felt very secure in this operation. He had even purchased a black Mercedes G500 SUV with dark tinted windows. Locals who saw his car on the street knew what kind of people owned this type of Mercedes. His G500 could be seen parked in front of local nightclubs on many late nights.

Compared to most of his local associates, his apartment was well furnished. The main room contained four large wooden dinner tables covered with computers and external hard drives. Sitting in one of the high back chairs with his face buried in a computer screen was Laslo, helper #1. He was taking long drags on his cigarette and typing very fast. As he exhaled, he slapped one hand on the table and yelled directly into the computer screen asking, "Edno, dve, tri....haresvali vi?" (One, Two, Three....Do you like it?)

Sitting in the chair next to Laslo, Georgi had been talking on a cell phone with Ivan in Moscow. He swiveled the chair to face his excited associate and motioned to keep the noise down.

Georgi was talking quietly and writing down numbers in a small notebook. As he finished his conversation and looked up, he said, "Mnogo blagodaria! Chao." (Thank you very much, goodbye!)

He turned to Laslo and asked, "How many dumps have you so far?"

After quickly typing another line of code into his computer, he responded in a thick accent, "Sir, we have now more than 28 million, including PINS on all debit cards, addresses and phones."

He continued to speak, "Their security service has no idea we are in the store's database. As this is week 3, and there are no alerts or issues, we can continue the progress on this system for much longer, maybe weeks or even months. I am receiving more than one million accounts per day at the present."

Appearing pleased, Georgi responded, "Magnificent. Process the encryption on the PIN codes and immediately send all batch files to Mr. Ivan's drop in Moscow."

At that moment, a soothing chime is heard from Georgi's laptop and on the screen, and a small window pops up showing a completed incoming Bitcoin transaction for 145 incoming BTC. ($26,461.35 USD) Georgi had received his weekly pay from BLR-Group.

From another laptop, the send Bitcoin message is visible. Completed and posted to the Block Chain.

Georgi turned to face the computer and opened a browser window for the BGAexchange.bg After logging in, he sent the full payment of Bitcoins into his account and placed a sell order with remarks to convert 45 Bitcoin into Bulgarian Lev.

Atlanta, Georgia

It had been a hot, muggy afternoon that August day in Atlanta. Jerry had spent most of the afternoon outside on the lot with potential new car buyers. New car sales at the Atlanta dealership had been superb this summer, and Jerry was enthusiastic about the future. It appeared that the American economy was finally making a recovery. The main crew on the sales floor in Atlanta were a hard working and hard partying group. Jerry had a taste for the younger girls but kept that a secret at work.

He lived in a studio apartment just outside of the Atlanta city limits. It had several laptops for his online use and five external hard drives where he stored his prized collection of Lolita images and videos. All of the drives were encrypted, of course, as he only used EncryptMeNow and the latest proxies to hide his activity from the prying eyes of the government.

His favorite girls were those with darker hair in the 7 to 10-year-old range. He loved outdoor shots and nature situations, like nude hiking. He thought to himself, what's the crime in photographing a beautiful naked eight-year-old girl. These scenes had accumulated in his memory and computer hard drives for over a decade. He knew his way around the dark areas of the Internet and the commercial

Lolita websites. Experience was a good teacher when it came to avoiding the government snoops. The seriousness of his child porn crimes had grown over the past decade, and so had his computer skills.

Tonight, Jerry was ready to try out a new private Lolita web, a destination; he had learned about in the chat rooms called, "Primal Young." As he entered his dingy studio apartment after work, he couldn't wait to get online and begin downloading photos. However, there was a problem in gaining access to the site.

This new Lolita web site did not yet accept Bitcoin. The operator was trying to look like a legitimate porn vendor and accepted cards through one of those offshore payment processors. Experience had taught him, those companies always promised a customer's name would be kept private, but he knew those listed often made their way to law enforcement. Jerry was taking no chances. Lolita porn was so risky, he knew even using one of those throwaway cards from the grocery store was too risky.

However, Jerry did have plenty of Bitcoins. He powered up his proxy network to hide behind, and logged into the carder forum, "Hotcards". The Russian guys always had quality dumps, and he could just buy some stolen cards to use for access to Primal Young.

He queried "Dumps BTC" that would point him to a seller that accepted Bitcoin. Right away, he found, Mr. Ivan & Friends, a well-known Russian dealer. He purchased six complete dumps and paid $140 in Bitcoin.

Moments later, Jerry had fresh stolen credit card information and an "alias" name to use on the new "Primal Young" website. Still on the same proxy, he downloaded the new stolen cards in a zip file and opened it on his other laptop. There were six freshly stolen VISA cards and six different people listed, each with the card number, expiration, CVV and a detailed listing of the card owner's address, and phone.

Mr. Ivan even provided the card spending limits that the bank had assigned to the accounts. After a long hot day on the car lot, he was going to enjoy the photos of young ladies and was now guaranteed to remain invisible by posing as one of these stolen card identities.

As he looked down the list, he found a card for Charles Martin, a resident of Great Falls, South Carolina. Not that it mattered, but when possible, he liked using identities from the East Coast. Stealing from his neighbors in the South made Jerry feel right at home. Plus, Charles Martin only had a $500 limit. Jerry always knew to use these cards first and quickly eat up the smaller balances.

Through no fault of his own, Charles Martin had used his card at one of the nation's largest department store chains. Unfortunately, the database storage located at the chain's headquarters in Ohio had been compromised and hacked over a month ago.

Jerry had just purchased Charles Martin's hacked card and identity information paying for it with Bitcoin. This card was now going to pay for a new membership on the "Primal Young" Lolita's website. "Thanks, Charles," he said aloud, "hope you like young girls."

Jerry knew that the card companies watched the IP addresses used by card holders, and he also knew of just the solution to beat the system. The same forums that sold the stolen dumps, often published detailed lists of proxies, for locations all over the US. The local proxies aided the carders that shopped online using the stolen cards. Jerry had learned this secret about six years ago after being declined across the board trying to use some stolen cards online. The proxies were a neat trick and just another tool in his Lolita arsenal. "I love the Internet!" he said aloud. Once again, Jerry powered up his VPN and proxy network.

Back on the carder web forums, a proxy located in York County, SC, was chosen. This County was an area just north of Charles Martin's residential address. Giving the appearance his computer IP address was located in that area, Jerry could then use that proxy to log onto the Lolita web and the online merchant processor would approve the stolen credit card transaction. Had he tried to make that card purchase through another far away city, region or country, the card processor would have suspected fraud and denied the purchase. He felt he knew all the tricks to staying safe online.

As Jerry found his way through the proxies and virtual private network onto the new kiddie porn website, he thought to himself, "How ironic, this web operator could have avoided this card fraud he just accepted Bitcoin."

Once on the website, high-resolution images of nude young girls in sexually explicit poses appeared inviting him to join. He typed in Charles Martin's stolen VISA card while connected through the local SC proxy, and the processor immediately approved the card transaction. The login screen for the new Lolita account, read

Thank you, Charles Martin, resident of Great Falls, logged in from IP XXX-XX-XXXX (York County, SC).

Jerry said aloud, "Perfecto," and began downloading nude pictures of his lovely Lolita underage girls.

Moscow, Russian Federation

> Важно не то, как долго ты прожил, а
> как хорошо жил.
>
> (How well you live makes a difference,
> not how long.)

Hacking US computers from Moscow was nearly a state-sponsored career. 4 of the 8 Russian's and 1 Bulgarian featured on the FBI Cyber's Most Wanted list, were working for Mr. Ivan.

Of course, Ivan was not his real name; it was an alias that he picked up long ago through BLR-group. The name had served him well, and he was known around the organized hacking world for selling quality dumps, bots, and financial data. During the last three years, his bot network and malware had raked in more than $153 million dollars selling stolen credit cards and financial data.

His BLR-group had more than two dozen low ranking "money mules" working for them. Their job was cashing out digital money. These stealthy locals used phony identities to "cash-out" Ivan's millions from transferred digital currencies, which flowed from the US, into the former CIS states.

The largest problem for Mr. Ivan's daily business occurred at the local "cashing" points. The end point in the dirty money route where they swapped digital funds into government currency was a risky deal. This point was the most dangerous and expensive part of his operation.

Burned into his memory was the American prosecutor who said, "If you want to catch these Russian crooks, follow the money trail."

It did not matter if the incoming money was euros, rubles or dollars, converting the digital currency into local national money was the most important job in his organization. Because of other players and gangs in the Moscow area, he was also on alert for rippers and thieves trying to steal the newly withdrawn cash. It was this part of his day-to-day operation where the money bottlenecks had always occurred.

Ivan had received his education in mathematics from Moscow State University. The Russian education system, which was originally established to focus on military-industrial careers, had been heavily weighted with mathematics. Because of this past concentration, Russian Universities had produced some of the world's greatest hackers.

In 2007, Ivan had been interviewed by a writer for a Russian magazine called, "The Hacker" and he was very proud of that feature article. Across the former CIS states, there were only about a dozen top hackers such as himself. Each of them knew and respected "Ivan".

He furnished his Moscow flat with older used furniture. He did not want anyone to find him living with very expensive furniture and luxury goods. He knew it was not good to make others jealous and show off one's wealth. The wrong associate may think he was making too much money and want a bigger slice of his income. He tried to play down his money. He had even purchased the smaller 5-series BMW instead of, the larger luxury 7-series.

However, one of the two bedrooms in his Moscow flat, stored new luxury goods his associates would buy with cash and stolen cards.

The carders working for Ivan had become very resourceful. Using stolen cards, they would buy expensive new release luxury goods online in the United States, such as handbags, and then ship them to Moscow from mail drops. Low-level carders working for Ivan often received the newest and finest athletic shoes, sunglasses, watches, clothing, jewelry, laptops, luggage, DVDs and electronic gadgets.

New movies on DVD were one of his favorites. Ivan loved American movies. Each year he received DVDs of first run movies still in theaters. A Russian associate, living in America, was able to get the Oscar nominated films directly from the studios in California, before the Oscar ceremony. These were films on DVD sent to the nominating committee members for review, and his American studio executive would sell them for cash. They would be shipped directly to Moscow by FedEx. Many local nightclub owners would request copies of his Oscar films.

He felt sure there was nothing he could not steal from the US.

He had packed the spare room in his apartment, floor to ceiling, with boxes full of luxury goods that he used as gifts and bribes around Moscow. Cash was always good for bribes, money always worked, but giving his landlord with the newest release of Nike sneakers, in his exact size, was much better than cash.

These luxury gifts had helped him to create many powerful friendships in Russia. He viewed the new Omega watches and LV (Louis Vuitton) handbags simply as a cost-of-doing-business in Moscow.

Ivan sat on his old couch counting a stack of US notes over the old wooden table in front of him. Next to the stack was a pile of Euros that also needed counting. After bundling up the US notes with large rubber bands, he began organizing and counting the Euros. Next to all the cash, sat three VISA gold credit cards. Each card had a different Russian name.

His iPhone rang. The call was short and ended with Ivan saying, "Yes, thank you." He stood and walked over to his ASUS Tech laptop on the dining room table. The screen showed a large gold

VISA logo moving randomly around, but as he began to type the screen saver disappeared. Now displayed on the laptop was a vBulletin Board template home page; its URL was bgCardershop.ru. The index page was a dark background with the yellow text headers. Once logged in, Ivan scrolled down to the section marked "Sell CC + CVV only". This section was a well-known carder forum section for buying and selling stolen credit card information or "dumps". Upon entering the section, he clicked on another, deeper level of the discussion labeled, "Track two." Ivan lit up a Marlboro Red cigarette and began typing several lines of information for new posts. He typed two posts in Russian and English under the username Mr. Ivan.

Post 1

Selling Fresh dumps, FULL, CC's + CVV

Accepting BTC, PM *(Bitcoin and Perfect Money)*

Only a second after he posted the offer, his laptop begins emitting a gentle tone and began showing new messages accumulating in his forum contact box. Before he could even enter another post, there were four messages from buyers wanting his newest stolen card data.

He began typing in his next forum post.

Post 2

Enroll, Shops, identity, matching dumps, addy, SSN

Enroll (COBs, Full info). Sell & Buy Accounts: Banks, PP, MB and more. Search SSN, DOB, Credit Reports, etc.

Accepting BTC, PM

Only moments later, the laptop again began to chime alerting him that his account had received several more messages. These were all buyers for his stolen card data. He opened each message and began typing responses. After several minutes, he moved the mouse over another program icon, clicked it, and the Bitcoin QT client appeared on his screen.

He hit the new address image, created a brand new wallet payment address and labeled it simply "Ivan". One more click brought up the new QR code. He then held up his iPhone and scanned the QR code saving it to a folder on his phone.

Back on the laptop, he highlighted the new wallet address, copied it and began posting it into each of the five messages responses. This wallet was the new Bitcoin address that would now receive payments from unknown users buying his stolen US credit card data.

Lately, Bitcoin had been his preferred method of receiving payments followed by Perfect Money. PM was a classic Russian system operated by criminals for criminals and most believed it to be untouchable by the US courts. Perfect Money had worked well for many years, but new customers all had Bitcoin, and they trusted the decentralized system. Western Union had also been very popular in Moscow.

Ivan's group supplied the money mules with new debit cards from a Chinese trade organization. He had been doing business with crooks in China going way back to the e-gold days. Chinese criminals were prompt and honest.

While the Chinese government continued to put out press announcements telling citizens, not to use Bitcoin, the local market for Bitcoin was booming.

As the government applied pressure to Chinese banks, which prevented them from doing business with Asian Bitcoin exchanges, these financial companies simply moved their bank accounts outside of China. Asia was the strongest market for Bitcoin in the world. The companies were always buyers of Mr. Ivan's cryptocurrency.

China, as it also turned out, was also one of the most corrupt places on earth. Daily cash bribes had always been a cost-of-doing-business in China. Most of that cash quietly flowed through nominee UnionPay debit cards. Over the years, many of these no-questions-asked Moneylink cards made their way to Moscow and into Ivan's hands. For many years, UnionPay had been supporting a reliable stream of cash flowing from Moscow area ATMs. This method, of exchanging Bitcoins through Chinese agents and withdrawing local money via UnionPay in Moscow, had always been exceptionally fast and safe.

Denver, Colorado

After BitStarter.com had forced the closure of Georgina's Bitcoin trading account, Mr. Green's was in trouble and quickly running out of cash. Millions of dollars' worth of Bitcoin sales had accumulated over the past few days and was just sitting in their Bitcoin wallet. Georgina quickly had to find a way to exchange the virtual currency into bankable dollars.

Disgusted with the nation's federal laws, she now looked outside of the US for a significant cryptocurrency exchange that could quickly sell the Bitcoins. She found BTC-Beijing. This company had always been a very successful global operation. If the company's central office in Beijing accepted her Delaware Corporation as a new client, she could immediately begin selling Mr. Green's massive inventory of Bitcoins and receive a wire transfer. This acceptance would ensure continued operation of Mr. Green's 4 Denver stores.

Georgina instructed the accountant in Delaware to complete and return the necessary signed corporate documents to BTC-Beijing, and they began selling Mr. Green's Bitcoins through Beijing.

Unfortunately, because of US regulations, BTC-Beijing was not able to wire the funds directly to any US bank. The company did not hold money transmitter license in any US state and had not yet registered with FinCEN.

Consequently, each day BTC-Beijing had to wire Mr. Green's settled funds to an account at a well-known bank in Singapore. After those daily funds had cleared, Georgina could have her money wired out anywhere she directed. Ultimately, this was right back to the Green Bitcoin Trading corporate account in Delaware. The account could then provide the necessary daily cash flow to all Denver area Mr. Green's Stores.

If this new bank workaround functioned properly, it would solve Georgina's Bitcoin sales issues, and Mr. Green's could then go back to selling legal Colorado marijuana. She thought to herself, "What a mountain of grief the federal government's old regulations had been causing her business!"

The last place on earth Georgina ever thought Mr. Green's Colorado profits would end up was in China! However, government regulations had left her no other possible financial options. Old federal regulations had forced her to move the entire Bitcoin exchange operation outside of the United States.

Fortunately for her, the Bitcoin proceeds took just a day to cycle through Singapore into the Delaware corporate account and the banks were working nicely with each other.

With the Colorado stores producing a steady daily profit, Georgina made it a point to pay back her start up loan. She wired $1.23 million dollars from the Singapore account back to her early investors. Those old friends in California, who had loaned her the startup capital to open four stores, were very pleased to have the entire loan paid back with interest.

Raqqa, Syria

Long ago, the precise definition of "money laundering" had been lost during the English to Arabic translation. Businessmen across Dubai, viewed "anti-money laundering" as an exclusively American program.

Original sources of funds always seemed to be just one fraudulent document away. Managers at Dubai trading companies had often been heard saying, "Let me make one call, and I can have that document for you." A thousand years of trading without banks had created an entire Islamic economy fueled by cash, handshakes and family reputations.

These agents bounced funding for the Islamic State from Qatar, Saudi Arabia, and other Gulf States, into the bank accounts of textile companies operating from the Jebel Ali Free Zone Authority. From there, the cash was mixed with other "legitimate" money swirling around the import/export economy of Dubai. Perhaps the funds were included in textile payments or circulated in gold bound for India. Whatever the scheme, after Dubai, the money appeared as part of a legitimate trading business. Those prominent officials, wealthy businessmen, and Arab charities, which were the Islamic State foreign funding sources, had been obscured from any direct link with terror funding.

The two Iranian brothers who operated the digital currency exchange in Dubai Internet City had been in business for more than a decade. They had a Commercial Brokerage License and were approved by the local government office. The brothers handled a majority of financial business through local banks in the UAE and also used other major foreign banks around the world. This hardened economic infrastructure handled direct wire transactions in US Dollars, Qatari Rial, Euros, UAE Dirham, Indian rupee and even Iranian Rial. The digital currency exchange operation also included local payment processors, Moneygram and direct connections to hawala networks in India and other parts of the Middle East.

After more than a decade in business, the only legal issue that had ever arisen in the company had been a series of humorous fines that the US government had levied on the company's American customers. A decade ago, the brother's original office was located in Kish Island, Iran. After a few successful years in operation, more than a thousand small US digital currency customers had been hit with civil penalties by the United States Office of Foreign Asset Control (OFAC).

Laughingly, these tiny retail Internet customers were accused of violating Iranian Transactions Regulations issued pursuant to the Trading with the Enemy Act. Unknown to them, laws prohibited American consumers from doing business with the beautiful tourist destination of Kish Island, which is technically part of Iran.

Unknowingly, thousands of American clients had been exchanging their digital currency into dollars through the Iranian (Kish Island) office of the brother's online exchange business. The American enforcement action had been typical of investigations that had taken place in the Middle East. US investigators regularly picked the low hanging fruit.

After the much-publicized enforcement action, the brothers had just removed the Kish Island address from their website and replaced it with a new Dubai office. Their successful digital currency business had continued to grow and prosper.

Amir had successfully received funding from an Arab charity in Qatar last month. This money flow is how value moved from respected Arab charities to the Islamic State.

The digital currency exchange office in Dubai had an incoming wire transfer of 859,377 AED, which had also originated in Dubai. After they had received these funds into the exchange company's local bank account, an amount of Bitcoin was transferred to an anonymous Bitcoin wallet address that was controlled and operated by ISIS associates in Syria. The brothers understood digital currency very well and recognized this as a pure trade based transaction. There was no possibility of the authorities determining who owned or operated the Bitcoin wallet and who was ultimately receiving the funds. There was also no way for anyone to trace the incoming funds that had been mixed together with trading accounts in Dubai. As far as the brothers knew, this large Bitcoin purchase had been another typical buy order. In Dubai, there was no legal responsibility to carry out a lengthy due diligence on any Bitcoin currency transactions, and consequently they never did. Amir had proven that he could effectively use Bitcoin as a direct legitimate funding source for the Islamic State.

Location Unknown

Bota's stolen Bitcoin mixed with dozens of other deposits to his laundry and over several days cycled through at least nine different transactions before emerging from his tumbler.

With the stolen 34,000 Bitcoins now clean and untraceable, Bota began to sell them through three major exchanges. Two of the exchanges were located in China and the third in Bulgaria. He would execute a series of smaller sells, perhaps 5,000 to 6,000 Bitcoin at a time through his two associates. He could then have the cash wired to his online casino accounts in Costa Rica in preparation for his next trip to beautiful San Jose.

Melbourne, Australia

Abdul had studied the Australian Government's public materials related to "combating terrorist funding". He was especially pleased, not to have found even one mention of the word "Bitcoin" in the Australian government's most recent report entitled, Terrorism Financing in Australia 2014. This document was published by the Australian Transaction Reports and Analysis Centre (AUSTRAC)

He had read the report cover to cover and never saw the word Bitcoin, and Abdul quickly recognized that when used anonymously, Bitcoin circumvented 100% of the transaction monitoring performed by the Australian banking sector.

Conventional bank based financial tools, which had been highly effective in identifying suspicious transaction patterns in the flow of a national currency, were useless in tracking funds moving through the Bitcoin system.

Bitcoin payments required no suspicious transaction reporting had no cross-border value restrictions or reporting, and best of all required no identification. He believed, as many others did, that when using the Tor network, it became impossible to supervise individual Bitcoin money transfers. Bitcoin's anonymous payment protection, also covered large value transactions with high-risk countries or known terrorist suspects.

Abdul realized that there was no method for any law enforcement organization to identify patterns of illegal deposits or money laundering across the Bitcoin network. In Australia, Abdul's friends started referring to Bitcoin as a "Digital Sandooq" (cash box).

Moscow, Russian Federation

As he finished posting the new Bitcoin payment address for a 6th customer sale, Ivan heard a knock on his apartment door. He picked up his cell phone and quickly slipped it into his pocket. When he opened the door, four gigantic men entered the apartment. The old wooden loft floor creaked under their weight.

Each man wore an elegant Italian leather jacket made by Schiatti & Co. Ivan recognized them because he had imported each one and given them to these businessmen as gifts.

The men had a looming presence and a very dark energy. Each man had a short haircut and Russian prison tattoos visible on their neck, arms, and hands.

Ivan greeted them and returned to his couch. He was not pleased to see them. Three of the men remained positioned by the closed apartment door and the other man, known only as Dimitri, walked over to Ivan. As he stood in front of Ivan, he said nothing and raised his hands as if questioning him. Ivan then reached behind the couch and retrieved a large LV bag. From the bag, Ivan removed two large packets of rubles and two stacks of euros, both were bound by thick rubber bands.

He handed these over to Dimitri and returned the bag. Obviously pleased, Dimitri quickly pushed the cash into his front coat pockets, tilted his head slightly and said to Ivan, "Ничего страшного." (No harm)

Unhappy about parting with his cash, Ivan sarcastically says, "Пожалуйста." (You're welcome) Ivan knew not to talk, or associate with this crowd. Last year, when one of their collections had gone wrong, in another part of Moscow, that crew had torn the head right off of the young criminal wannabe that could not pay.

These colossal men were not top criminal minds in the Bratva; these were mid-level collection agents. They were bag men for the real businessmen that ran Moscow. However, when they arrived for a regular cash pickup, that person better have the money. No payment would mean that this person was guaranteed to spend the next few unconscious months in the Sklifosovsky Emergency Institute, which was the principal trauma and emergency hospital in downtown Moscow. About once a month, Ivan heard of someone around town ending up at Sklifosovsky.

As Dimitri turned to leave, one of the large men positioned by the front door, reached into his pocket and pulled out a handwritten note. He handed it to Dimitri, who then turned and handed it back to Ivan.

Dimitri said, "для моих сестер, спасибо" (for my sisters). He turned and again they all began shuffling out the door.

The notepaper contained a list of luxury goods that Ivan was to get for Dimitri. Thugs often made requests for expensive luxury goods that they then lavished on the girls working in local clubs. He knew that Dimitri did not have any actual sisters or even any family. Ivan understood that because of his global connections, he was to provide them with these expensive luxury gifts and not ask questions.

As he closed the door behind them, Ivan politely said, "За здоровье, Будем здоровы!" (Cheers, let's stay healthy)

By this time, Ivan's laptop was again beeping which signaled more incoming buyers and more Bitcoin.

He returned to the laptop and began typing. There had already been 19 different incoming Bitcoin transactions posted through his QT wallet, and the balance was growing very rapidly. He removed his smartphone and again scanned the QR code that now appeared on the laptop screen.

The 38,000 dollars of incoming funds, now safe in the mobile wallet, would shortly be moved through China onto UnionPay cards.

Part 3

<u>Atlanta, Georgia</u>

That evening, Jerry had been very pleased with the fast connection speed of his new Lolita website and had been busy viewing pictures and downloading the ones he liked.

Primal Young was similar to the many underage database sites. The structure of the site, involved levels of participation. Knowing how to navigate the website was important with kiddie porn sites. 100 to 120 pages could be accessed by new members at the entry level. The pictures each hid links to the next level, which was about 100 more pages. Not everyone understood how the Lolita operators hid and disguised their best images and videos. Jerry knew this topic very well. Each picture, which he clicked, that did not open a new larger image, would take him deeper and deeper into the web structure. At each level, he had to continue clicking other new images in order to find entrances to the deeper level of content. This test kept out the soft core visitors who were just on the site for a quick thrill. The hardcore users like Jerry had always found their way deep into the site's content. The deeper a visitor went, the more hardcore the images became.

When Jerry got to the next level, he noticed the URL change. As the photos in level three began to appear, he saw links to 300 more pages with images on this level. As he had started clicking the pictures, the 7th image had connected him to a new URL and the next level of depravity that contained both photos and videos.

At each URL change, the deeper levels offered up more and more "engaging" content, and he was quick to download as much as possible. He would spend a week or two, sorting and categorizing his new acquisitions.

When he reached the final 4th level, the URL again changed and had offered him a downloadable zip file full of "new" images and Lolita videos. "Jackpot," he thought to himself. This purchase was offering 1.8 gigs of zipped photos and videos at a cost of $179.00, and it was only payable in Bitcoin. As he clicked the download link, he was forwarded to a file sharing website based in New Zealand where the file had begun downloading. Once complete, in order to receive the password that would unlock the zip file allowing access to all the goodies, he would have to make an anonymous Bitcoin payment of $179.00.

He opened his TrueEncryption software and clicked "Create Volume", then selected "Hidden TrueEncryption Storage Volume" and created a hidden private disk storage area nicknamed "Primal Young." This folder was an eyes-only, storage volume, and he was sure to hide it from discovery. If anyone ever got a hold of his backup drives, they would not be able to find or access the files encrypted on the drive.

Moments later as the download finished, he was returned to the original website, and the screen generated a new Bitcoin address for the $179.00 payment. Jerry opened his Bitcoin QT wallet, copied and pasted the wallet code and completed his payment. A 25 digit alphanumeric password appeared which he copied and saved to Roboform.

He smiled, knowing it was going to be a long night.

Louisville, Kentucky

> Being a criminal is not a skill you can learn in books, and it's not a career you want to start later in life. ~ Ace

Bubba sat, drinking beer from a can, in the double wide trailer, directly across from the front door. No one entered or exited, without his official permission. Bubba's real name was Donald, but at 360 pounds, everyone just called him Bubba. As Ace's cousin, he had been hired to handle security for the trailer and Ace's nightclubs around Louisville. No one lived in the double wide, and, no one ever visited the trailer, except Ace, his banker Franklin and some of Ace's redneck criminal friends.

Ace and Franklin had been in the back bedroom, talking to one of Ace's redneck criminal friends and showing off his businesses.

73

Ace said, "We just maintain the enormous database of images, we don't create any pictures or even process payments unless they are in Bitcoin. Right now, that card processor in Belize is taking payments for us on some "junior" sites, we have good bank connections in Belize. My cousin Ricky went down there last year and had no problem moving the cash in and out. They are backwards down there!" he said with a condescending laugh.

Ace continued talking, "Mostly, we have been using Bitcoins. No more Western Union. Nope, nothing except crypto. The world is pushing us in that direction. We are serving a digital future. Buy a prepaid digital cell phone, load it up with anonymous digital money and spend it on our Lolitas. Digital currency is the best thing that could have ever happened to the Lolita porn business. Anonymous digital payments."

Ace had always liked to show off his business to local rednecks and other criminals throughout Kentucky and Ohio. They all knew how much money Ace had made and the strip clubs he owned.

Seated in a rusted folding chair, more towards the front of the trailer was Franklin, one of Ace's employees. Franklin was resting his bones in front of a large flat screen monitor covered with digital ledgers that were part of a professional accounting program. In the right-hand corner of his screen, a very distinct Bitcoin QT wallet program was visible.

Franklin was the official "banker" for all of Ace's businesses, a sort of in-house criminal accountant. He was in the trailer each day overseeing the online kiddie porn business and at the clubs each night moving the money. All of the dirty kiddie porn funds were mixed together and cleaned through the Ace's local strip clubs and an assortment of other semi-legitimate businesses throughout the region.

Bubba thought Franklin was a bona fide redneck criminal genius. Every day, he engaged in financial business in faraway places like China and Bulgaria. Ace's dirty money ran through strange financial companies, registered in places Franklin had called "Banana

Republics". Bubba never understood what was going on in the trailer.

Franklin had been busy working on one of the computers and quickly adding up numbers with a large handheld calculator he had purchased one Christmas Eve at the Radcliff Kmart back in the early 1990's. He and Bubba used to go to the Kmart at least once a week shopping, and then eat at the Long John Silvers in the front parking lot.

From the back bedroom of the trailer, Ace began loudly bragging about his operation to the tattooed redneck standing next to him, "We have, over half a million downloadable Lolita images we sell online. They are priced by the piece, the batch or a membership subscription at $79.00 for 20 days.

Bitcoin makes all this possible using these here anonymous proxy transactions. We hide; they buy! We even keep our Lolita images on another company's servers. Franklin there hacks into the servers, uploads the files so when it's time to sell; the pervs are downloading them from some clueless "straw" company. Last year, we were using a stationary store, in Canada for five months straight! They had no clue. It was beautiful. Other times we hide the Lolita porn in with the regular porn on someone else's porn servers. Their bandwidth, their servers, their headaches.

We do some credit card processing through Central America, but as I said before, these are not the payments on our hardcore girlies, credit cards are trouble. Right now we are clearing about $280,000 per month in Lolita cash, and most of that runs right through our clubs.

Do you need a new car? We just bought the Eastern Kentucky Car auctions, get you a new car when you need it, and we'll be running some cash though there too."

Ace tapped Franklin on the shoulder and asked, "What are we doing with that incoming Bitcoin?"

Franklin sets his calculator down the turns to Ace, "It's real slick, this batch, we are running through three or four wallets and into the tumbler."

Ace asks, "The Bitcoin Laundry machine?"

Franklin answers, "Yes, that disguises it and the boys can't track it back to our business. No one knows where it came from, and we sell the fresh Bitcoin though our primary exchange guys in Bulgaria and China. The whole sales transaction gets spread out over four days, but it's K-L-E-A-N clean. Wires go to our Swedish bank account, and it's ready to use."

Ace responds, "Ok, Franklin, let me know when this batch is done." Ace then turned to his redneck friend, who was mesmerized by all the information and said, "We're even working on a new line of Bitcoin debit cards, trying to get them working in the clubs. They come from Singapore. This digital stuff is nothing short of a criminal's wet dream."

Ace went on to say, "Franklin, pull up that new site, we are running, Primal Young, show that to EB."

As Franklin moved to another computer and began typing, both Ace and EB shuffled in for a closer look. The index page became visible, two small naked girls, appeared, and some text was inviting the visitor to join.

Ace again began talking, "Now, see this site is dirty and has lots of little girls on it, but it's not the hardcore stuff we usually sell. This website is what we use to entice the perverts. These images bring them into our network. There, we sell them the high dollar Lolita stuff. There are four places on this web, where we link to the hardcore stuff, and each connection sells images and zip files loaded with the explicit material. The kiddie videos are real dirty and we spread we spread it out over the Internet. 90% or more of the visitors that register here using a credit card will buy at least one of our Lolita folders full of images. 90%! That's where all this Bitcoin comes from! We put up one of our zip files, and Franklin here chats about it in the perv forums. We can pull in 300,000-400,000 dollars in a week before the boys catch on and take it down."

Ace and EB now look back to Franklin working on another nearby laptop. That screen shows the sale of $140k in Bitcoin to the Chinese exchange BTC-Beijing.

Beverly Hills, California

Larry was on the phone waiting for Todd to pick up.

"Hello, Larry, how can I help you?"

Larry says, "Todd, the last wire has now gone out to you, it is 17 total. When do you want me in there?"

Todd responded, "Larry, give us three or four days, and we can meet on Friday if that works for you, how about 3:00?"

Larry tells him, "Yes, that works for me. I'll see you in your offices on Friday, thanks very much."

Tel Aviv, Israel

It was not his real name, but, "Dr. David" had created and now operated the GreyMarket, a Darknet Bitcoin drug bazaar, and Bitcoin banking system. He had been a software engineer based in Israel for the past decade. Ever since the Darknet and Bitcoin had merged to form a perfect union of online dealers, Dr. began to see opportunities in this emerging industry. The doctor felt he could do a better job of facilitating these nefarious online connections and had set out to create the perfect global narcotics marketplace.

The GreyMarket now boasted more than 4,000 listings. While the GrayMarket permitted sales of anything, a majority of the customers were selling drugs. Never in the history of civilization had so many powerful recreational drugs been so accessible to people around the world.

While again praising Bitcoin for making the world a better place, Dr. David perused that day's 109 new listing. The quick list showed:

GreyMarket / Drugs /

1. 1 GR AFGHAN #3 HIGH QUALITY HEROIN HIGH QUALITY This is heroin brought from Afghanistan. It has a very high degree of purity, can be smoked or injected.

2. 25 tabs Diazepam. 20mg each

3. 12 tabs Nitrazepam 5mg each

4. 50 tabs Anavar 25mg each

5. 0.5 GR AFGHAN #3 HEROIN HIGH QUALITY

6. 2gms Anhydrous Cleaned Cocaine [High Purity]

7. 5g (Na-GHB) GHB Crystal Block

8. 3.5g High Quality/Purity Speed Paste - Dutch A++

9. 100 Oxymorphone (Opana) 10mg IR (Red Generics!)

10. 8 x Adderall XR 25mg FE

11. Fentanyl gel Patch 50mcg (Watson) - Next Day

12. 3.5g - Psilocybe Cubensis Golden Teacher

13. Potent Pot Chocolate Chip Cookies (a dozen)

14. 0.5gm ORIGINAL COLOMBIAN COCAINE AAA++++ FREE SHIP - Cocaine is one of the purest in the world. This cocaine can be snorted, smoked and injected.

15. 0.5gms Heroin

16. 7.5gms Original Indian Hash AAA+

17. 15gms Original Indian Hash AAA+

18. Blue Dream - 56 grams (2 ounce) - Indoor

19. 25 ml of Shaw's greatest GBL(99.9%)

20. 1x 25i-Nbome Acid 1000ug Blotter

21. ChemDawg Brownies, Legendary (one dozen, free shipping)

22. Testosterone Propionate 100mg/mL 10mL Bulk up.

23. 50 DBOL (Methandrostenolone/Dianabol) 25mg (we ship USA)

24. Liquid Anavar (oxandrolone) 50mL bottle 25mg (overnight shipping)

25. Deca Durabolin (Nandrolone Decanoate) 300mg/m (we ship USA)

26. MASTERON 100mg/mL Drostanolone Propionate (we ship USA)

27. Testosterone Enanthate 250 mg/mL 10mL

28. 50 Winstrol (Stanozolol) 25mg tabs

29. Equipoise 200mg/mL 10ml bottles

30. 50 Anavar (Oxandrolone) tablets, 25mg each.

31. HCG 5000 I.U. Human Chorionic Gonadotrophin (we ship USA)

32. Etizolam Powder 1g

33. 28g Blue Crack (AAA+)

34. Ketamine/Amphetamine purity test kit I only have one please

35. 4x 25i NBOMe 1200μg HPBCD Acid blotters

36. 1g Ethylphenidate - Meth analogue (best iv)

37. 1 litre- 1,4 butanediol 99.9% reagent grade AAA+

38. 7g Premium GDP Honeycomb Wax

39. Fentanyl 100microgram patch

40. DOC 5mg Blotter tabs

41. Heroin 1 Gram - Straight off the brick, but will be crushed to powder for shipping and stealth purposes. This is introductory price since I'm new here.

42. Gun Powder Heroin

43. 2mg Xanax Bars

44. This listing is for 0.5g or half gram of #4 heroin.

45. 1g of Cocaine

46. Black Tar Heroin

47. 1 gram- *ICE* [Crystal Meth]

48. BLACK TAR HEROIN

49. 1.0 Gram of China White Heroin

50. FISHSCALE Cocaine (Uncut)

51. 60mg MS-Contin (Generic ABG)

52. 1 gram of MDMA from Amsterdam

53. 1g Bubba Kush

54. DJ Shorty E Blue Berry Kush

55. 1 GRAM PURE MDMA

56. MDMA Molly Grade A x 1g

57. A-PVP 1g - substitute for coke, adderall, meth, or crack

58. 1gm Cocaine Grade A+

59. 1 Gram A-PVP Powder (Pure)

60. XXX OG only

61. 10mg dextroamphetamine tablets, Barr

62. Premium High Quality Crystal Meth - shards

63. 100x Etizolam Blotters 1mg each ~Stealth~

64. 3.5g (8th) of White Berry OG

65. DJ Short E Blue Berry Kush

66. 10 Grams MDMA imported from Amsterdam

67. 50g crystal MDMA -FE SPECIAL LISTING

68. 5g crystal MDMA - White & Tan

69. 2.5gms Dutch Top Shelf Quality Weed

70. 100 x 25C-NBOME Blotters 1000ug each

71. Viagra generic (sildenafil 100mg) 100 tablets

72. 5 pack of XTC pills from Amsterdam

73. 1G HQ PURE SPEED PASTE 72%

74. Cocaine Grade B x 4 gram

75. Blue Dream - 28 grams (1 ounce) - Indoor

76. Blue Dream - 3.5 grams - Indoor - Soil -Fresh

77. 25 Grams Ethylphenidate

78. 7.0g Mix/Shake (AAA+)

79. Provigil generic (modafinil 200mg) 100 tablet

80. 4gms INTERNATIONAL FE REQ Cocaine Grade A+

81. Busbar (Buspirone) 10mg

82. 100 tabs. Winstrol 20mg

83. 3.5g Grape Skunk (AAA+)

84. A-PVP 7g sub for crack adderall meth speed

85. 7.0g Green Crack (AAA+)

86. 3.5g Skunk No. 1 (AAA+)

87. 25g ~ Colombian Brown Sugar•#4 Heroin

88. 32g - Mescaline containing San Pedro Cactus

89. Ayahuasca Three Person Kit

90. 7.0g Blueberry Cough (AAA+)

91. 3.5g Medical Grade Cannabis

92. .5 gram 4-ACO-DMT Fumarate ~Stealth Shipping

93. 25 x 25C-NBOME Blotters 1000ug each

94. 3.5g White Widow (AAA+)

95. 7.0g Violator Kush (AAA+)

96. 7.0g Hindu Kush (AAA+)

97. THOMPSON-SPEED PASTE 10g+++HIGH QUALITY+

98. 1g Sample Swazi Gold Outdoor African Sativa

99. 1g 90%+ Pure Crystal Meth Ice Shards

100. Cialis generic tadalafil 20mg 100 tablets

101. INTERNATIONAL FE REQ Cocaine Grade B x 8 gram

102. 50 Bugatti XTC pills (200mg MDMA content)

103. Methocarbamol 500mg

104. 100 pack of XTC pills from Amsterdam

105. 3x 15mg oxycodone OC stamp

106.	3g Shroom puck
107.	12 tabs. Nitrazepam 5mg
108.	50 tabs. Anavar 25mg
109.	25 tabs C20 Diazepam. 20mg Diazepam

All new listings, paid the Dr. a fee and once the item sold, another commission fee was collected. Since opening the GreyMarket, Dr. David had earned more than $4,400,000 in Bitcoins.

Lagos, Nigeria

Mabry was an online scammer and computer expert. He operated out of Lagos, Nigeria. In earlier years, he had been one of the largest 419 operators in the country. However, these days, he ran High Yield Investment Programs (HYIP Ponzi investment scams). The online scams sold phony investments claiming to be either Forex trading, commodity players or a Bitcoin expert trading in and out of the markets.

It had been hard to make a profit in this HYIP business since the demise of digital gold only a few years earlier. However, Bitcoin had come along and replaced centralized online currency. Cryptocurrency again made online High Yield Investment Programs simple and anonymous.

About six years ago, while running several larger HYIPs, Mabry had discovered an easy way to multiply his HYIP profits. Today, using this method, he was simultaneously operating 18 different online HYIPs.

The two tricks for profitable operation were to stay online as long as possible before folding up the investment and always to accept enormous payments, not small change. Bitcoin investments of $10,000 to $50,000 were not common. However, whales did occasionally surface, and when it happened the HYIP operator had to take notice and act.

The hallmark of any successful HYIP Ponzi scam was to appear legitimate by staying online, paying interest as long as possible. Mabry had figured out that it was beneficial for the operator to be running many HYIP Investments at the same time. Using this method, funds from several smaller HYIPs could be pooled together and make payouts to other HYIP programs. This system gave the larger programs legitimacy. As long as the investors in one HYIP were being paid, more funds would keep flowing into that scam and his pocket.

In the long run, operating multiple HYIP scams at one time was much more profitable.

Several of his so-called "investment" programs had been regularly bringing in cash throughout the past year, which caused Mabry to branch out into additional scams. He had taken some of his Bitcoin profits and purchased a batch of stolen credit card BINs. Consequently, while running his investment scams, he had also been carding merchandise online. Stolen credit cards were everywhere in Nigeria.

Raqqa, Syria

Hawala is a traditional Islamic method of financial transfer embraced by Muhammad.

"Praise the Prophet for the good that he has done and for the status that Allah has given him," Amir said aloud.

Hawala transfers left no visible paper trail. Thanks to the hawala networks, all previous years of funding for the Islamic State and its affiliates, which came from Opium sales and other business elite, had quietly flowed through hawala networks.

After recently identifying the many post 9/11 bank surveillance programs from leaked NSA documents, digital currency had suddenly become an attractive option for the Islamic world. Using Bitcoin, long distance funding support for the Islamic State could flow effortlessly around the world. Amir continued, "We ask Allah to hasten Bitcoin's usage for us."

Unlike earlier years when face-to-face recruitment occurred mainly through religious schools, Amir understood that today's Jihadist recruiting took place online. Amir and other Jihadists across the Middle East, already had sophisticated knowledge of the Tor network, experience using powerful encrypted email services such as the European Tutu-privi system, and were even known to use the new Blackphone.

This new Bitcoin virtual currency had proven its worth to the Islamic State. Mobile Bitcoin Wallets controlled by Amir, had just received more than 850,000 AED (+$200,000 USD) in Bitcoin funding from Islamic Charities in the Gulf Region. With these Bitcoin donations, Amir would bolster the already successful Islamic State social media campaign and online video recruiting operation. Amir sent the Bitcoin into a tumbler, which further disguised their origins, and began to set up new wallets which would be used to forward the digital cash on to global affiliates in the Jihadist network.

Once back from a tumbler, the Bitcoins were instantly transferred to Islamic State affiliates around the world, including those in Africa, Asia and the United Kingdom.

This Bitcoin funding would allow them to purchase new computers, burner cell phones and HD video recorders. These tools would greatly improve the Islamic State's media and recruitment efforts.

Amir, immediately executed Bitcoin transfers to Lagos, Nigeria, Putrajaya, Malaysia, Mindanao, Philippines, London, England, Canberra, Australia and Jakarta, Indonesia. As Amir, pressed the last send button on the Bitcoin QT program, transferring funds to associates in Jakarta, he said aloud, "Praise be to Allah and peace and blessings be upon the Messenger of Allah." As there were many Bitcoin currency exchanges already operating in each of these countries, all of the Bitcoins would quickly and anonymously be converted into local currency.

Moscow, Russian Federation

Mr. Ivan sold millions of stolen credit cards, debit cards, and online bank logins. However, this was not his core business. Ivan was world renown for his malware and bot networks. His most recent network had grown to control more than 4 million computers. It had widely distributed his malicious programs around the entire world. This malware allowed his workers to steal money from corporations, retirement accounts, personal bank accounts, brokerage accounts and college savings.

He had cashed out entire stock portfolios from hacked US brokerage accounts, often waiting for settlement, then wiring out the balance into dummy bank accounts.

Over the past two years, Ivan was proud to note that his Russian bot networks had compromised over a billion online financial accounts.

One of his favorite thefts had been the member bank accounts for a large American city's Police Pension Fund. His bank-based-botnet had gained access through their website, and then produced the individual bank account access for more than 30,000 active Police officer members and 65,000 retired members of the city's Police force.

Having obtained logins, passwords and digital signatures for these bank accounts, Ivan had transferred the bank balances, "on behalf of the account owners" into the accounts of shell companies he controlled.

After raiding the primary pension bank accounts, he then resold all of the member's personal bank information on Hotcards.ru forums and earned another large pile of Bitcoins.

Referring to Ivan's global bot network, a special agent of the FBI had made this statement in a newspaper interview, "Financial cyber crime, such as this bot network, poses a significant threat to our country, threatening our national security, our financial security, and our privacy."

In Moscow, he would have never attempted such a theft against the Russian police forces. He believed that in Moscow if Department K had caught him stealing from the American Police, they may have awarded him a medal!

The card BINs had turned into a very profitable business over the past decade. However, Ivan felt that banks around the world may soon have no alternative except to stop using cards in favor of a decentralized payment system such as Bitcoin.

He questioned, "How long could the American merchants continue paying the 3, 4 or 5% transaction fees and live with the massive amount of card fraud? How long could the American banks continue to operate with these size losses?"

Ivan's latest incarnation was a powerful update of an old Trojan program he created. Hackers called the software by many names such as CryptoLocker, BitCrypt, Zerolocker and others. Ivan had originally written this Trojan program to infect a user's PC and steal all of the Bitcoins from operating cryptocurrency wallets. It had been so successful, that he repackaged the bug and added a "ransomware" program. His group had been selling the primary program on forums for many years and today it was in use around the world.

The new updated more powerful version of the ransomware, encrypted only the necessary files on a compromised user's PC and required a Bitcoin payment within the first 48 hours after being infected. He charged a modest 3 Bitcoins for the ransom, and then once the victim had paid the ransom, he promptly provided the correct password key to clear and unlock the program. He had always thought of himself as an honest criminal.

The ransomware froze about 60% of the unprotected computers around the world which became infected. The software then blocked users from accessing almost all necessary files. 99.9% of these victims quickly paid the full 3 Bitcoin ransom.

This scam was a splendid money maker for hackers because it was relatively easy to get the bot onto a user's PC. The aggressive encryption produced a powerful RSA-2048 key specifically for that one infected computer.

In order to seize a personal computer, the bot only required 9 seconds to install itself. After that moment, the ransom clock started ticking!

Seattle, Washington

Lexi climbed out of the beat up, 2008 Nissan and told her friend behind the wheel to wait in front of the bar for her return and keep the engine running. She entered the dive bar neatly carrying an Acer laptop under her arm.

It was the 5:00 o'clock on a Friday. That was cocktail hour, and all the Seattle regulars were already buzzing on their second pitcher of cheap beer.

As she made her way to the back bar, she immediately saw Noah sitting at the far end with his laptop open. She approached Noah and leaned into where he was sitting and quietly said, "I need 30." Noah acknowledged her comment and pointed to a nearby empty table. Lexi moved to the table and sat down.

Noah's laptop screen now showed a Bitcoin wallet. The text on the display was in Chinese, and the denomination of the balance showed in Yuan. Noah then clicked an icon on the bottom of his screen, and a small calculator appears. He plugged in some large numbers, then moved back to the wallet where he again typed in the same large number. The account showed almost 200,000 yuan worth of Bitcoin, which now appeared in another part of the portfolio, signifying that a considerable amount of Bitcoin had moved from one wallet to another.

"DJ Lexi" was famous in the Seattle rave scene. She wasn't an actual DJ; it was an honorary title that she had earned by delivering moly to the best parties and raves in the area. She supplied both the moly and meth, and after she had arrived, the party kicked into high gear. She was a mid-level seller often buying up to a kilo of product and reselling smaller bulk packages.

In reality, Lexi had been a real nerd most of her life. After high school, she had been a waitress, bartender and even one of those medical test subjects for a nearby lab company. She loved computers, and in 2010 had been immediately attracted to the Bitcoin and the darknet. Both her laptop and her phone had excellent encryption, VPNs and a selection of overseas proxies.

Her DJ career had started when the Red-Path online drug bazaar opened. The Red-Path, was a darknet website, only accessible through the Tor network. Since it began, years ago, the online market had ballooned in size and selection of drugs. She had been buying moly in bulk online through Red-path for over two years. It was the best moly in the country, perhaps the world and she bought it by the kilo. She broke it down to ounces and quarter pounds, then resold it to local friends and dealers. She was making about 9,000 dollars a week in profit on the moly, then came the meth. Since bulk prices had emerged on Red-path, her meth sales had skyrocketed. Never before, had such high-quality drugs been so accessible and available online, or anywhere on the local scene. Before Red-path, she never could have purchased a kilo of anything, at the street level. The online drug bazaars had opened up a world of high-quality bulk drugs for her and anyone else that knew how to access the Darknet and pay with Bitcoin. With her local connections and Bitcoin experience, she had quickly become a player in Seattle.

She sat quietly at the table in that Seattle bar for about 5 minutes, then, with his laptop open, Noah sat down and joined her. He spoke first, "$34,500, is your total tonight." Lexi then reached into her coat pocket and pulled out two rolls of US cash. "Here is 35 and I'll be back tomorrow." Noah took the money and turned his laptop to face Lexi. With the QR code clearly visible on the screen, she took her iPhone, touched the screen twice and held it over the QR code. She heard a small beep. As she pulled her phone back, she looked at her laptop screen and confirmed that the transfer was complete.

Lexi said, "Thanks, man, see you tomorrow."

She exited the bar and walked to the waiting car. As they pulled away from the curb, Lexi again opened her laptop, inserted a USB 4g WiFiwire prepaid modem and began connecting to the Internet. Traffic slowed, and the rush hour crowd started to accumulate on the street in front of the Nissan.

On her laptop, Lexi engaged the local WiFiwire connection, then opened the Tor browser. The browser window showed a small green onion shown at the top of the screen.

The car moved slowly through downtown Seattle traffic. Now, connected through the anonymous Tor network, Lexi clicked a bookmark then a long URL appears in the address bar. It was a seller page from the Red-path drug bazaar. She scrolled down the page and clicked on a broad picture of the drug moly.

The page in her browser read, "Moly Drogen Shop Mit Bitcoins online bestellen".

Further down the page there were a series of radio buttons. Lexi clicked the 1000gram radio button and her shopping cart then showed (1) item. She opened the now full Bitcoin wallet, which Noah has just loaded $34,000 in Bitcoin from the bar and continued with the checkout process.

She selected a radio button for shipping that read, "DHL Paket (mit Tracking, mit Unterschrift - auch für Packstationen): 16.00 €" then began typing a local Seattle address for delivery.

The final checkout payment screen, then appeared. It reads:

Checkout

Thank you. Your order has been received.

- Order: **#48724**
- Date: **07/09/XXXX**
- Total: **26847.76 €**
- Payment method: **Bitcoin Payment**

Sende die Zahlung EXAKT (oder mehr) wie folgt /

Please send your bitcoin payment EXACTLY (or more) as follows:

Amount (**BTC**):   **93.0691**

Address:

16bYwmubKtHkktr2z32mthyfthMy7FAd22

Bitte beachte / Please note:

1. Du musst die Zahlung binnen einer Stunde abschicken! Ergo sende die Zahlung nur von deiner eigenen Wallet aus! / You must make a payment within 1 hour, or your order will be cancelled. Please do not send from any 3rd party wallets as they might delay the payment.

2. Sobald die Zahlung bestätigt wurde, wird der Status deiner Bestellung auf "in Bearbeitung/Processing" geändert und schon bald versendet. / As soon as your payment is received in full your order status changes from "On-Hold" to "processing". Your order will be shipped as soon as possible.

3. Sofern ihr bezahlt habt, seid ihr fertig. Bitte fragt nicht blöd nach ob alles in Ordnung ist, ob die Zahlung ankam etc. ... // If you've paid you're done. Please do NOT ask if everything went fine or if the payment was received...

Order Details

Product	Total
Cart Subtotal:	15005 €
Shipping:	16.00 € via DHL Paket (mit Tracking, mit Unterschrift)
Order Total:	15021 €
Shiny-Flakes MDMA 86% purity × **1**	15005 €

In welcher Größe möchtest du dein MDMA?

Product	Total

In which size do you want your MDMA?:

> Steine (Rocks)

Customer details

Email:

> DJLex@mysecuremails.net

Billing Address

Jane Smith
XXX XXXXXX Avenue

PO Box XXXXX

Seattle, WA 98124

With the screen now showing the payment QR code and address, Lexi highlighted the address then cut and pasted it into her Bitcoin wallet. She had sent $19,016 dollars in Bitcoin to the seller.

Noticing the activity, the driver asks her, "How much are you getting this week?"

Lexi responded, "Another kilo, but his prices are rising for the fast US delivery. $19,000."

Lexi then clicked another bookmark on the browser window opening yet another seller's page in Red-path. She scrolled down and again clicked on 1 kg, and completed a similar checkout for the second time, sending $9600 in Bitcoin to another seller.

Lexi says, "We can make it up on the cost of the ice from our west coast meth guys."

The driver then asks, "Did you buy enough Bitcoin to cover it tonight?"

Lexi smiled for the first time that evening and said, "Yep, the world runs on Bitcoin."

The driver also smiled and quickly responded, "Yep, THE UNDERWORLD!"

They both laughed as the car moved down the crowded roadway.

Portland, Oregon

After Joaquin's pickup in Vancouver, he called Clarisa and let her know there was another $10,000 in Bitcoin available to liquidate that evening.

Great Falls, South Carolina

Charlie had lived his entire life in South Carolina and his entire adult life in the small town of Great Falls. That Thursday, he was busy working at his full-time job in the Walmart warehouse, when his supervisor and two men wearing suits approached him.

Showing off the new tie that Charlie had given him as a birthday gift, his supervisor approached him and said, "Charlie, these men would like to talk to you."

Charlie placed the box he had been carrying on the floor, removed his gloves and turned to greet the men. "Hello," he politely said nodding to the first man. As he repeated the gesture with the second man, they said nothing and advanced on Charlie.

The first man circled around Charlie's back, while the second man began speaking, "Charles Martin, you are under arrest for violation of U.S. Title 18, Chapter 110, section 2252, the purchase and possession of Child Pornography."

Shocked by what the man had just said, Charlie asked, "What?"

As the first agent pulled Charlie's arms behind his back and placed handcuffs on his wrists, Charlie again questioned, "What are you doing?"

He said, "I'm FBI special agent Irving, and this is FBI special agent Washington. You are being arrested for the purchase and possession of Child Pornography, which is a violation of Federal Law US Title 18, section 22512."

Now in handcuffs, Charlie fell to his knees, "No, no, I don't understand, I love children, this is wrong."

While four other Walmart warehouse employees appeared behind him, Charlie's Walmart supervisor, who has been standing about 15 feet away, now looked on in horror.

With his hands cuffed behind his back, Charlie balanced on his knees as the agent began to read his Miranda rights, "You have the right to remain silent when questioned. Anything you say may be used against you in a court of law. You have the right to consult an attorney before speaking to the police and to have an attorney present during questioning now or in the future. If you cannot afford an attorney, one will be appointed for you before any questioning. If you decide to answer any questions now, without a lawyer present, you will still have the right to stop answering at any time until you talk to a lawyer. Do you fully understand these rights as I have read them to you today?"

Special Agent Washington now pulled Charlie to his feet and again asked, "Mr. Martin, do you understand these rights?"

Loudly crying Charlie responded, "Yes, I think so."

The two agents then began to escort Charlie out of the warehouse area through the store. Charlie's Walmart supervisor asked, "Where are you taking him, what has he done?"

Agent Washington responded, "Purchase and Possession of Child Pornography. You won't be seeing him for a long time."

As dozens of shoppers and employees watched in shock, the two agents lead Charlie crying in handcuffs, through the entire length of the store. He stumbled from the back warehouse, up the central aisle, past the Subway restaurant counter and out the automatic front doors.

Charlie was so confused and embarrassed he could only hold his head down and sob as they exited the store.

Pearl District Portland, Oregon

Since his 30th birthday, Riley had spent the last eight months, designing and producing his new Bitcoin ATM machine. This shoebox-sized vending machine accepted cash and dispensed Bitcoins.

This Bitcoin ATM concept was not new to the world. There were several companies that already commercially produced Bitcoin ATMs, however, those ATM units were gigantic and expensive. The companies producing those machines had taken an existing bank ATM and converted it to dispense Bitcoins. The units were bulky and very expensive.

A few other companies in the marketplace sold homemade machines that looked suspiciously like an early 1980's jukebox.

Riley's ATM was small, about the size of a Gumball machine and connected securely to the ground using an excellent metal stand that a friend in Portland had manufactured out of recycled metal. This machine, like most others in the marketplace, connected to the Internet using a local WI-Fi signal.

Riley's new Bitcoin ATM was one of the smallest units in the world, and it was packed full of convenient features. Since beginning mass production of these machines in a rented Portland garage, he had sold 14. Six of these units were operating in the Portland area, and he had shipped six units to Denver for use in the new legal Marijuana dispensary stores.

Anyone could walk up and use the ATM machine. The compact size meant there were no build outs such as a palm vein reader or an image recognition camera for ID verification. The unit had no tools for customer identification or due diligence, it just accepted cash and transferred Bitcoins.

He laughed as he said to himself, "License-Shmicense. We don't need no stinking money transmitter license!"

His ATMs were very popular with the local Portland crowd and while the largest size US bill, it accepted was a $20, there were no maximum transaction limits. If a walk up customer wanted to feed a $1000 into the machine, then they could purchase that much Bitcoin. Riley felt that placing restrictions on a Bitcoin purchase was a ridiculous idea.

While the unit held just 10 Bitcoins in the local hot wallet, the process to refill the wallet was almost instant. The machine would create an alert as it neared a zero balance in the hot wallet. The alarm triggered the ATM's computer it to connect automatically to the primary exchange in Bulgaria anytime the unit needed to refill the hot wallet.

If a customer inserted $300 and the machine needed Bitcoin, it merely made the Internet connection and pulled Bitcoin from Riley's account at the exchange. After Riley had sold the ATM, it was independently operated; the business owner connected a Bitcoin trading account that maintained their balance that fed the ATM operation.

For Riley, the big money and continuous income generated by these machines did not come from the transaction fee. The big profit was made buying Bitcoins slightly below the market then feeding the machine the cheap coins. Riley was always buying Bitcoins from local and friendly sellers. He could then pay below the market price and earn that extra income.

As people bought Bitcoins from the ATM, it would sell those coins at market prices. If Riley could continue buying coins at 10% below the market price and resell them higher, he could retire at age 40. Riley was always on the lookout for more Bitcoins from local users at a discounted price. He even solicited some of the businesses that bought machines from him, the machines he operated always needed more Bitcoins.

His most popular Portland machine sat neatly in the corner of a popular coffee house on Hawthorne Blvd. Eighty to one hundred people visited the shop daily, and the machine was doing an enormous cash business.

Riley was also about to deliver on another order of 20 machines for a Seattle operator, who planned to install them in bars and restaurants around the city. Riley attended the local Meetups in Portland and often bought Bitcoin from the attendees. He recognized that cash talked, and the locals were willing to sell at off market prices, meaning he could buy Bitcoins for cash at a discount. He would immediately load them into his ATMs and deposit the balances in his Bulgarian trading account. As the machines sold the Bitcoins, he generated a good profit for himself.

He also bought Bitcoins through connections from the website, mylocalbitcoins.net, which paired buyers and sellers living close to each other. His cash came in through the machines and mostly cycled back out buying Bitcoins locally. This process was a real cash intensive business and consequently, his profits and his activity were off the books.

Atlanta, Georgia

On the nineteenth day of his online Primal Young membership, Jerry was ready to collect all the images he could, and then drop this fake persona and move on to greener pastures. He always wanted more girls for his collection and had located a Primal Young address for another one of the "special" zip files he could purchase with Bitcoin.

He had been actively searching for new pictures, deep inside the Primal Young web structure and found one more large zip file that contained both hardcore Lolita pics and videos.

Today's first zip had been easy to find. That file had contained just the hardcore pictures, and it cost $129 in Bitcoin. The second zip, costing $219, included both the pictures and videos. Jerry did not have enough Bitcoin to cover both purchases, so he chose the large video inclusive package.

He clicked the "Purchase with Bitcoin" link and Tor browser forwarded to a file sharing website where his download immediately began. The file was easy enough to find and download. However, he needed to complete the Bitcoin purchase in order to obtain the password that would open the encrypted file. He continued with his purchase, opened his Bitcoin QT wallet, cut and pasted the wallet address then hit send. After he had completed the Bitcoin payment, a new page opened on his monitor, with a 25 digit password. He quickly copied into the Robo password saver, and Jerry sat back waiting for the complete file download.

Louisville, Kentucky

Franklin's computer screen now showed an incoming Bitcoin transaction for $219 in Bitcoin from a blank Bitcoin wallet address. Franklin looked briefly at the display, then began punching numbers into his giant Kmart calculator.

Ace had been entertaining another of his criminal cohorts in Bubba's trailer. This man was named Harris. He imported tons of Marijuana from Canada each month and distributed it to three states. Harris had served almost 17 years in prison and was not as "tech savvy" as many of Ace's other associates.

Ace was saying, "You see, Bitcoin is an untraceable version of electronic cash. Everything we can do with untraceable cash, we can now do with the Bitcoin."

Harris asked, "When you sell the Bitcoin for dollars, where does that take place?"

Ace responds, "China and Bulgaria are the biggest and most trusted services, and they are both way outside of the US."

Harris, "How to you get the Bitcoin out of the US and into the foreign exchanges."

Ace responds, "Are you retarded Harris, haven't you heard anything I've been telling you? Bitcoin is an Internet payment system. It takes just two seconds for me to transfer a million dollars from my Kentucky Horse Farm to Beijing, China, no questions asked."

Harris again asks a redundant question, "Ace, don't the banks want to know where the funds came from?"

Ace again, "Harris, the banks are not in the loop, all of this runs over the Internet and we hide behind these here proxies and the Tor. The regulated banks don't even know we are alive, and we are going to keep it that way."

Harris, "I'm running money mules over the border each week with less than $10,000 in cash and you telling me, that the government don't see any Bitcoin moving in or out of the US? You don't have any customs border hang-ups?"

Ace again retorts, "Fuck no, partner. This crypto flows around the world in seconds with no ID requirements, no maximum restrictions and no tax reporting. Did you hear that? We don't have to fraud up any tax returns when we use Bitcoin because the banks don't have any record of it. Digital currency is 100% off the books. Just like running shine, this is off the books. This here's the future son."

Harris, "Electronic cash... now they got restrictions on how much US money can cross the border, but they got no laws on how much Bitcoin can cross the border? Damn, I'll be. We got to start using this stuff with my boys in Cincinnati and up north."

Motioning towards the door, Ace says, "Harris, come on around back, I got us a jar of Red's shine. Come on we can have a nip."

Tel Aviv, Israel

GreyMarket was more than just another Darknet market. Dr. David was a very skilled software designer and had created an entire Bitcoin banking service within the market. As security had always been a prime concern in the handling and storing of customers' Bitcoins, GreyMarket delivered significant improvements in safety and transaction efficiency.

GreyMarket would accept Bitcoin deposits from customers, hold them for at least 6 verified confirmations and then permit the movement of Bitcoin from one account to another in off-market transactions. Bitcoin deposits were updated every 8 minutes and new funds appeared as balances in the system after just 2 confirmations and were then cleared for trading after 6.

As the Bitcoins moved through each in-house GreyMarket transaction, the blockchain held no record of the movement. In essence, this was a private marketplace. The movement of funds only occurred through the market's server and was hidden from the outside world and the blockchain. Consequently, after depositing Bitcoin, there was no possible way to trace any GreyMarket transaction through the blockchain. Many GreyMarket vendors found this quite inspirational.

After depositing Bitcoin, if a client sold a pound of Cocaine or a kilo of Meth, no outside record of the transaction was even visible to the public through the blockchain. Additionally, being an off-market trade, the Bitcoin transactions cleared instantly, none of the GreyMarket in-house operations ever required any confirmation through the Bitcoin platform. This additional layer of privacy preserved and promoted customer trust in the GreyMarket system.

Of course the initial depositing and final withdrawals of Bitcoins were always transacted through nicknames and pseudonyms, no personal information of any kind was ever used. Dr. David also ensured that all of these outside transactions were free of charge.

The movement of funds from in-house sales had created a beautiful stream of fees for Dr. David. He was charging $0.02 per transaction, plus an additional 2.1% of all total amounts transferred. If any customer bought or sold an item and Bitcoin moved inside the market, a transaction fee was generated and paid to the Dr.

This was David's bread and butter. His marketplace had more than 30,000 active members and business was epic good!

User accounts were offered optional automated multi-sig or centralized escrow.

A multi-signature transaction created a multi-signature address for sending funds. The primary reason for using this strategy was to cut down or prevent the theft of Bitcoins. This type of sale provided protection for both the vendors and buyers.

As an added bonus for members, all shipping fees were segregated and paid in full to the sellers. Dr. David ensured that his vendors saved on shipping costs and he felt this was a point missed by many other Darknet drug markets.

Bitcoin withdrawals could be made anytime and were processed at the top of each hour 24/7.

In successful escrow transactions, the Bitcoin funds, within the GreyMarket system, were automatically deposited to seller's wallet the moment a buyer released them. Along with a fully integrated internal messaging system, inventory management and an easy-to-use dispute center, the Dr.'s system had proven itself to be the most efficiently run Darknet drug market on the Internet.

Typical of any online marketplace, GreyMarket had a seller reputation system. As more positive comments were received and the seller proved to be reliable, less and less escrow transactions were required.

TorChat and PGP were both recommended and widely used. A PGP key was used on 99% of all transactions. Every transaction was labeled, prior to a sale, to show if PGP or Escrow was required.

All disputes could be investigated and resolved through the in-house moderator. Most users tried to avoid disputes because this process generated another healthy fee for the Dr.

Inside GreyMarket, sellers received a free customizable store. Customizable banners, colors and fonts were all available to sellers at no additional cost. In order to properly market goods, the Dr. felt that all items listed through a seller should appear in their storefront. Items could be pinned or featured, specials and discounts could be added and it was even possible to create a coupon for special users.

Through GreyMarket, Dr. David had built a world class global drug bazaar, surpassing any comparable legitimate eCommerce website.

Seattle, Washington

It had been a great night for Julia and Steven. Their Bitcoin mining had again produced a generous profit for the month. They now had a total of $22,000 of cash in the house. She had bought a small fire safe to hold the money. This purchase had made Steven happy, but they both acknowledged that anyone could simply pick up the safe and steal it, as they had not bolted it to the floor.

With Steven still asleep, Julia was awake in the kitchen starting her morning routine. It was still dark out as she began to brew the coffee. Suddenly, she heard what sounded like a window breaking. The window in her living room, covered with egg cartons, was being smashed. As she turned to see what was happening, a small canister fell, from the broken window onto the living room floor. As she took a step towards the window, still holding the coffee pot, she felt an intense blast as her living room exploded. There were deafening noises and a blinding flash from the area below the window. She dropped the coffee pot and immediately fell to the ground. Smoke began to blanket the room while a loud ringing filled her ears. A moment later, she heard another loud crash, as the front door broke open. Then she saw the men entering her home.

It was the King County Sheriff's Emergency Response Team (ERT) also known as SWAT. To her surprise, officers with assault weapons pointing at her, were now piling into her little home Through the ringing in her ears, she heard them yelling. "Sheriff's department, search warrant, King County Sheriff's department, search warrant on the ground."

Moments later, as she lay face down on the kitchen floor in handcuffs, she saw Steven, still wearing his boxers, being dragged out of the bedroom in handcuffs.

Buenes Aries, Argentina

Miguel lived and worked in Buenos Aries, Argentina. He had been in retail sales most of his life and now at 58 years old he owned and operated a medium sized clothing store offering goods for both men and women. It was mostly a cash business until two years ago, when his nephew had convinced him to begin selling clothing online. His online clothing sales had been very successful, and now the web store outpaced his local shop.

One of the biggest online expenses in Miguel's sales was the currency conversion. Sales to the US and Europe were all denominated in dollars and euro. The post-sale conversion of dollars and euro into the Argentine peso had become an expensive transaction.

On top of this expensive issue, inflation in Argentina was running more than 3% each month. It was no longer safe to leave funds tied up in the peso. Consequently, earlier that year Miguel had begun accumulating Bitcoin and holding the virtual currency in place of the peso.

This Bitcoin investment plan had been working out very well for Miguel's finances. He had also found a new start-up Argentinian company that would process all of his online credit card transactions in dollars and euro, and then pay him in Bitcoin.

Back in 2012 the government had passed an amendment that barred consumers and businesses from using PayPal. For the past several years, Miguel's payment options had been limited. Bitcoin had developed into a fantastic option for enterprises in Argentina.

The new payment processor gave him a low flat percentage fee for each card transaction and did not charge for converting the national currency proceeds into Bitcoin.

Since Bitcoin prices had been increasing over the past two years, his holdings were now very profitable. Using Bitcoin allowed him to live in Argentina, transact his global clothing business in dollars and euro, and then receive the proceeds in Bitcoin. This entire equation now took place completely outside of the Argentinian financial system.

As an Argentine businessman, he recognized that Bitcoin was a new platform for growth and opportunity. Additionally, there was a significant local Bitcoin exchange now opening in Argentina.

Portland, Oregon

After dropping Clarisa off, a few blocks from the post office, Jenny headed over the river to the Bridge Lounge, the site of this week's Tuesday night Bitcoin Meetup.

The Bridge Lounge was the first business in Portland to accept Bitcoin. The owner of the bar was a real nerd, and he figured that it would help his liquor sales and also promote Bitcoin. He even bought one of those neon "Bitcoin accepted here" signs that hung in his front window. Next to the neon was the "Bathrooms are for patrons only" sign written with a magic marker on beer-stained paper.

Jenny's job, while living in Joaquin's house, was to chauffeur people around town as needed and sell the Bitcoins for cash. She attended the Bitcoin Meetups in several local cities besides Portland and made a ton of contacts through mylocalbitcoins.net. Bitcoin sales had been splendid!

After parking, she grabbed her laptop from under the front seat and headed into the lounge. Inside, she immediately noticed, Marty, sitting in the booth farthest from the bar. He saw Jenny and tried to wave as she turned away and headed straight for the bar. Her priority of the night was always a cold beer. After taking a few sips, she walked back towards Marty. He was the go-to-guy for most Bitcoin transactions taking place at the Meetup. Marty sat with his laptop open taking notes on a bar napkin. He said, "Hey Jenny, how are you tonight?"

Jenny placed her beer down on Marty's table opened her laptop and sat down.

Anyone buying or selling Bitcoin at the Meetup was smart to first talk to Marty. Trading Bitcoin was his full-time job, and he was an expert at creating local market liquidity for anyone needing to move cryptocurrency.

She opened the conversation with numbers, "I've got 25 to sell tonight, and maybe by closing time I'll have another ten."

Marty responded with, "Great, let's talk price."

Unfortunately, Marty had not grown up in Juarez, Mexico, where Jenny's family had resided. His negotiating skills were somewhat weak.

Jenny said, "Marty, we go through this every week, you start low and I go high. Can we skip the small talk tonight, I'll give you my 25, perhaps 35 by evening's end at 3% below the quoted price on the Bulgarian market. Cash talks Marty, and there are going to be a big crowd of buyers here tonight. I think I saw Alexandro pulling up as I came in…."

Marty responded, "Ah, Jenny you are correct, tonight's Meetup will be crowded, but judging by my earlier emails, they will all be sellers. I can go 8% below, BTC-Beijing's price, which I believe is now higher than Bulgaria."

Jenny tells him, "Well, it's always great doing business with you Marty, but I'll have to stick at 3% and just take a look at the market prices later tonight. I'll be shooting some pool over here for the next two or three hours and entertaining buyers at 3% off, give me the signal when you are ready to buy."

As she stood up and began to walk away, her cell phone rang. The caller was Joaquin. He wanted to confirm that he had just transferred in another 10,000 dollars in Bitcoin that could now go up for sale.

About an hour into her pool game, Jenny was approached by a familiar buyer named Riley. They began talking, and as it turns out, Riley agreed to purchase 35,000 dollars of Bitcoin from Jenny at 4% off the market.

She laid down her pool cue, grabbed her laptop and followed Riley to a booth. From across the room, Marty caught a glance of Jenny and Riley talking and shaking hands over the table.

Riley then reached into his jacket pockets and pulled out two brown lunch bags, thick with US currency and passed it over the table to Jenny. He said, "There is 10 in twenties, and the rest is hundreds."

She accepted it, then obscured from view; she began to count it quickly on the bench seat next to her purse. About 10 minutes later, she looked up and said, "Ok, all good."

Jenny opened her large leather handbag, which had been resting on the bench seat, moved her loaded Glock 9mm to one side of the bag, and placed the money deep into the purse below the weapon.

She then opened her laptop and raised her iPhone. She typed a few keys on the computer, then touched her iPhone screen and used it to scan a QR code on the laptop screen. She heard the familiar tiny beep that signaled the transfer. She then turned her laptop to face Riley. Seeing the new QR code, Riley moved his phone over the code for a quick scan. She heard another beep, then Riley began to review the smartphone screen. He nodded to Jenny in the affirmative and said, "Thank you, can we do the same amount each week?"

Jenny responds, "Yes, I have minimum 25, max 35 in Bitcoin each week, no problem. Thank you Riley."

Riley said, "Superb, thank you and have a pleasant night."

Only moments after Jenny's sale, the front door to the bar opened and in walked Brian Simpson with his 15-year old daughter. The bar was off limits to children, but during Meetups, everyone gathered in the back banquet room, and they permitted kids at the meetings.

Brian was a well-dressed programmer in his late 30's. His young 15-year old daughter was bubbling over with excitement to be at the Bitcoin Meetup and further exploring the world of digital money. The two immediately began moving towards the famous new Bitcoin ATM. At the table, there were three people in line before them, so they waited and watched as the small machine ate $20 notes and dispensed Bitcoin to happy mobile phones.

By the time April and Brian made it to the machine, April was bubbling over with excitement.

She said, "Dad, this is it. It's the newest Bitcoin ATM machine, and we can buy Bitcoins." Unaware of the unit's significance, Brian said, "That's great honey, how much are we going to buy?"

April responded, "$100 worth." Brian reached into his pocket, removed his money clip, and carefully passed five twenty dollar bills over to April. "Now make sure we get our Bitcoins and don't lose the cash."

April frowned and said, "Daaadddd."

Unfortunately, for April the machine was now signaling that it was out of Bitcoins.

She turned to her father and said, "Oh, no the machine is sold out." Hovering nearby, Riley heard her statement and interrupted the pair saying, "Don't worry, I will load it up again. When the machine is in full-time use, it can call up the exchange and reload itself, but tonight I have that feature disconnected."

Riley then leaned over the machine with a key and opened the back of the metal box. After touching several keys inside the machine, he maneuvered his iPhone over the machine's camera, and he heard a familiar beep. He then gently closed the lid, locked the back and moved aside. He said to April, "Now you are all set, I have loaded the machine with fresh new Bitcoins. Thank you for trying out my ATM."

Moments later, April began feeding the 20 dollar notes into the ATM one at a time until they were all gone. Then, she raised her iPhone, touched the screen twice and held it in front of the unit scanning the QR code presented on the machine's tiny screen. She suddenly heard the beep and that caused April to jump as she exclaimed, "I got it."

As she looked her phone's screen, she noted that her new Bitcoin wallet balance was now $118.74. The ATM had added hundred dollars in Bitcoin to her mobile wallet. She turned to her dad and showed him the new balance. Pulling the iPhone back close to her chest, she told her father, "Let's go shopping!"

Buenes Aries, Argentina

Miguel's online store sold over 3,000 different items. The company that provided his software was a homegrown version of Shopify. This business had allowed any Argentinian merchant to set up and operate an store online. The company did not yet permit Bitcoin transactions through the software, but Miguel felt confident that soon Bitcoin would be accepted. His nephew had customized his online store using the Argentinian flag and local photos. Miguel had paid his nephew for his work in Bitcoin.

Bitcoin had become a savior to Miguel's business and many other local companies across the region. In some nearby markets, Bitcoin was so desirable that it sold at a premium to the global market price. Trying to stock up on Bitcoin, local cash buyers would regularly pay 40-50% over market prices. As more people adopted the currency, that activity had driven up their local prices.

Pearl District Portland, Oregon

The smell of fresh bread filled the bakery as April, and her dad entered. The Main Street Bakery near Brian's condo in Portland accepted Bitcoin and for the past few days, April had talked about spending some Bitcoins in the shop. Brian followed April through the front door and as they approached the counter; a lovely young woman covered in tattoos greeted them.

April asked, "You accept Bitcoin, right?"

The young lady responded, "Yes, and using Bitcoin, instead of plastic, we give you an extra 5% off your total purchase."

Brian responded asking her, "That's great, why do you give the discount?"

The clerk replied, "Bitcoin saves us money in credit card processing fees, and we pass those savings on to our customers."

Brian smiled and responded, "Outstanding, I didn't know that."

April tugged on his arm and said, "See dad, I told you."

The clerk follows up asking, "What can I get you today?"

Brian said, "We need two of the multigrain whole wheat hearth loaves, uncut, a dozen of the almond croissants." Now pointing to the case in front of them Brian declared, "Two of these cupcakes, it's a long walk home!"

The clerk moved towards the whole wheat bread, calmly responding to Brian saying, "Perfect, 44, 36, 10."

Totaling the order for Brian the clerk said, "That will be $90 even and with your 5% discount that comes to $85.50." She then touched the screen of her iPhone several times and entered the amount. As a large QR code appeared on the iPhone, she held it up displaying the code for them to scan.

April now held her iPhone over the QR code, and again, a tiny beep was heard, which again caused her to jump a little.

As April pulled her phone back, she turned to her dad and said, "See, one day all payments will be made with Bitcoin!"

Brian responded, "If you say so honey."

As the clerk passed the bags of baked goods over the counter, she also gave Brian a postcard sized piece of thick paper. On the front of the card appeared an advertisement for the bakery. The card's back showed the image of a physical gold Bitcoin with text reading, "The World Runs on Bitcoin."

Brian smiled and said, "Thanks, I like it."

Part 4

Lagos, Nigeria

Later that afternoon, Mabry's front door slammed open and four gun-toting men stumbled into his tiny Lagos apartment. The heavily armed men did not concern Mabry, as he recognized the second man to be Sadracko, his brother.

Sadracko was a deadly gangster in Lagos. He had been arrested in the United States years earlier and shipped back to Nigeria, where, after a large bribe, he was released to continue his criminal career.

As the door closed behind them, Sadracko spoke through a mouthful of Khat, "Mabry, my brother, you must help me. My crew and I have kidnaped an extraordinary man, and we must receive and launder the ransom money for this party." As Sadracko continued to talk, the seriousness of Mabry's situation became more and more apparent.

Soccer was the national sport in Nigeria, everyone, including the President, attended the games. The most famous player on any the team was the vice-captain, Joseph Remy. He was a beloved Nigerian and the team's highest scoring player.

Isaac Remy, just happened to be Joseph's young brother and two days earlier, while returning from a nightclub, Isaac, had gone missing. The television news had been showing pictures of him and asked for any information on the disappearance. Online, Mabry had also noticed that every modern Nigerian newspaper, TV station, blogger, and Bitcoin user was saying awful things about the kidnappers.

The local press reported that the kidnappers had made a bold request through an unsigned email containing their demands. It reads:

We demand $100,000 US Dollars, which must be paid to our Bitcoin wallet or we will plunge a knife into Isaac Remy's heart. We will call the family in 24 hours and tell them the method to get our Bitcoin wallet number.

After that, you will have 24 more hours to make the payment. Do you want Isaac to live? Then pay us.

Sadracko now continued to speak, "Mabry, we have kidnaped Isaac Remy, Joseph Remy's smaller brother. We need to collect the ransom money and put the Bitcoins into your tumbler, so there are no tracks back to us. We asked for the payment in Bitcoin; you must help us to move the ransom money through Bitcoin. You are the expert, I know this… Mabry, it is US $100,000 US Dollars, and I will give you some."

Mabry was in shock that his brother, Sadracko, had kidnaped a family member of Nigeria's most beloved football player. He sat down on the couch and raised his hands as if to ask God forgiveness.

"What have you done?" said Mabry. He paused, shaking his head and then said, "Oh Lord."

Sadracko again spoke, "Mabry, we have asked for $100,000 in Bitcoin, can you convert this to Naira for us once paid?"

Mabry knew that his brother Sadracko had never owned a computer and could not even comprehend how to operate a mobile Bitcoin wallet. He quickly realized any involvement from him, even at the smallest level, would put Mabry along with Sadracko squarely in the middle of a national kidnapping crime. Mabry would undoubtedly become public enemy number one.

He immediately stood up, waving his arms towards the front door and said, "Absolutely, not. I want no part in this. Get out, get out now, and let Remy's brother go free."

Sadracko grabbed his brother's shirt and pulled him in close, "Mabry, bro, you owe me, you must help us?"

Again Mabry protested, "No, I will not help you. Where is Issac now?" Sadracko motioned towards the apartment door and said, "He's in the boot of the car."

Mabry said, "It is 103 degrees, and you have him in the boot?"

Showing some anger, Mabry yelled, "Get out, I want no part in this." He began to push the groups of armed men out of his apartment and onto the street. After they had moved passed the entranceway, Mabry slammed and locked the door; he wanted no part in hurting Joseph Remy. The man was a national hero.

As the sun rose on the next day, the TV news reported that Remy's younger brother had been released by his captors and was home again safe and sound.

Great Falls, South Carolina

It had been 116 hard days before Charlie obtained release from the Federal Detention Center on bond. After walking out, he had to take a 5-hour bus ride back from Estill then on to his tiny apartment in Great Falls.

As he finally stepped off the number 4 bus in front of his apartment complex, he felt relieved to be home. Turning the corner between the buildings, he saw his apartment for the first time since his release on child pornography charges.

The metal front door had a massive dent near the handle, where the Sheriff's battering ram had forced entry. The wood door frame was shattered and splintered into tiny pieces. There was police tape across the wood frame in 6 places blocking entry.

The crushed door, could not close on its own. It was being held shut by two large red stickers placed there, also by the Sheriff's office, declaring the residence off limits.

The front window that opened into his kitchen was missing its screen, and someone had spray painted the letters F-A-G in red paint on the outside of the storm window.

Charlie was too tired and too angry to cry.

The police tape came off easily with one swipe of his hand. He took out the 3" long yellow stub pencil that he had saved from his time in lockup, poked it through the red stickers on the front door and entered the dwelling. Somebody had ransacked his tiny apartment.

112

They had pulled every item he owned from the kitchen cabinets and closet shelves. His computer and television were missing. The few belongings he owned were now thrown on the floor and scattered throughout the place mixed with open cereal boxes and dirty socks. The cushions on his sleeper couch had been cut open, and the word PERVERT was spray painted on his living room wall.

Weak from his journey, Charlie fell to the floor. Twice he had been severely beaten while in lock up. The second time, inmates had tried to rape him. He had fought them with all of his strength. After that second assault, his battered face and eyes had been so swollen he could not see anything for two days.

Now, on his knees in the apartment, he saw a pile of mail and documents in the floor space next to him. Sorting through the pile, he found an eviction notice dated 25 days ago, a letter from Walmart terminating his employment and a letter from his bank stating that they had closed his account.

Through no fault of his own, the life he had, which had been so wonderful, was gone. Whoever had stolen his credit card information, had caused his downfall.

The things he loved, the people he called his friends, and the only place in the world he had ever lived were now all gone.

Suddenly, Charlie's mind froze. He had a moment of clarity like no other in his existence.

While removing his leather belt, Charlie stood up and walked to the closet.

Looping his thick leather belt over the wooden beam, he hung himself.

Beverly Hills, California

Larry had returned from an excellent dinner with friends. After being served, his soon to be ex-wife, had moved out several days ago. The Nanny was caring for his new son David in their guest house. His home, which had witnessed two prior divorces was again peaceful and quiet.

"The world was in order," he thought to himself.

As he entered the home, his office phone could be heard ringing in the back of the house. Ignoring all after hour's call was typical for Larry, he would just check the voice mail in the morning.

Larry headed to the bar. His right hand poured while his left hand held the crystal glass. With a large glass of Johnny Walker, he sat down in the living area just off the kitchen.

As the TV came on, he again heard his office phone ringing. While the kitchen TV volume was on mute, the late KTLA news was showing clips from the California Attorney General's office. The headline reads; Beverly Hills Bitcoin Ponzi Scheme busted. The news caught Larry's attention, and as the station went to commercial, he reached for the remote.

Again the phone in his office began ringing, however, this time he ran and answered it. He wondered who would be calling the business line at 11:20pm on a weeknight. Larry answered, "Hello."

It was his lawyer Bernie Levine. Bernie responded, "Larry, I got you. Have you seen the news?"

Larry responded, "Bernie, I just walked in and poured a drink. What is this story about Bitcoin?"

Bernie then asked, "Larry, did you give your funds to Todd Smith, the accountant?"

Larry said, "Yes, the transaction concluded days ago."

Bernie asked, "Larry, how many days ago?"

Larry counted on his fingers with his left and said, "Bernie, it was 12 days ago, what's going on?"

Sounding hysterical, Bernie now said, "Oh my God, Larry, how much did you give him?"

Larry responded, "Bernie you said you had vetted the guy, and I could trust his firm. I wired a total of 17 million dollars."

Bernie then said, "Oh shit. Larry this guy, Todd, and his firm were running a massive Ponzi scheme using Bitcoins, and he has fleeced half of Hollywood." Bernie continued to talk, saying, "Apparently, he fled the country two days ago into South America, and they can't find him or anyone's money… or Bitcoins."

It now hits Larry that Todd scammed him for the full $17 million, and the shellfish he had for dinner immediately came up covering the Zeigler Mahal Persian Carpet in his office.

Wiping his mouth, he said to Bernie, "No that can't be, my money is safe in cold storage, NO, that can't be, and we must reverse the wires. Can't the bank trace the funds? Bernie!"

Bernie said, "I don't know Larry, eleven other clients of mine had similar arrangements with Todd. This is bad, really bad."

His hand was now shaking, Larry again reached for his drink and turned to one of the flat screens in his office. Again, the news broadcaster started talking about the case.

Standing a block from the office of Todd A. Smith and holding a thick stack of court papers, the reporter began talking, "The indictment surfaced this afternoon, but it was too late to apprehend Todd A. Smith. He had already fled to South America on a private jet out of LAX with all of his clients' money. Police detectives and FBI agents are now combing through the offices of Allen, Smith and Cohen right here in the heart of Beverly Hills. Todd A. Smith, a California attorney, and accountant had been operating a sophisticated Ponzi investment scheme using a virtual digital currency known as Bitcoin."

"Shit," said Larry as he took a big drink from his glass and collapsed into his office chair.

Switching through the channels, he found the story on every local news station. The next channel had a report standing next to the Beverly Hills offices, only a few feet away from the other reporter.

He began by saying, "The indictment alleges that for the past 15 months, Todd A. Smith, a partner in the firm, convinced more than thirty of the firm's wealthy clientele to place funds with his high yielding Bitcoin investment scheme. The scheme, however, had no real method of producing any income. Two lucky, investors were paid back with funds from incoming victims in the last weeks before the scheme collapsed."

Now yelling, Bernie says, "Last weeks, that was my money, that's when I wired my $17 million, give me my money back. Bernie, get me the names of those investors."

As if a light bulb went on in his head, Larry now begins shaking his head side-to-side as if to say, "Nope that won't work either."

With his head hanging down, Larry now speaks into the phone, "Bernie, how am I going to claim $17 million of my money is missing? I just filed divorce papers with the court, without listing that money as an asset."

Seattle, Washington

That afternoon, Lexi had been surfing through the Tor network. She had burned through more than two dozen new drug market websites checking prices, quality feedback, and delivery terms. She also had bookmarked some the places for investigating later in the week.

The last web she visited had instantly started a download on her computer. She tried to disconnect as quickly as possible but had not acted fast enough, and the software had just installed itself.

Moments later, she found her computer had frozen and would not function. "What the fuck?" she said aloud. After trying to correct the problem by hitting control-alt-delete, she gave up and went to see Noah. If anyone could figure out the problem, it would be Noah the computer genius.

After a few minutes of looking at her non-working laptop, a big smile covered Noah's face. "You downloaded the Bitcoin ransomware. The bug locked up your files until you pay the ransom!" he said.

Lexi responded, "What the fuck, how can that be?" As Noah turned the computer back on, he held down the ESC key, and a new screen appeared.

The text reads:

"Your personal files are encrypted on this computer: photos, videos, and documents. The process of encryption has produced a unique public key, RSA-2048, generated only for this machine. To decrypt the files, you need to obtain the private key. The single copy of the private key, which will allow you to decrypt your data, is located on a secret Internet server. The server will automatically destroy this key after a time specified in this window. After that, nobody will ever be able to restore your computer files, and they will be lost forever. To obtain the private key for this particular computer, which will automatically decrypt all of your records, you need to pay money to us. Any attempt to remove or damage this software will lead to the immediate destruction of the private key by server."

Private key will be destroyed on July 24 at 1:22am.

Time left 45:40:06

You must pay 3 Bitcoins to this Bitcoin address. 1N9SN3vAArSwYjQixuBBiTKDsNJtRgnAab

<<Click here to pay 3 BTC>>

As the program scrolled down a new page appeared.

It contained text and instructions to make the payment required to free up the computer.

Lexi said, "Holy shit, I have to pay these crooks 3 Bitcoins to get my computer back?"

Noah replied, "Yes, this Russian ransomware is serious stuff, they are distributing it across the Tor network. Were you on Tor when you downloaded it?"

Lexi said, "Yes, it scammed me into the download."

Noah, "Ok then, just pay the ticket and get your computer back. You've got Bitcoins on your phone."

Unhappy about it, Lexi continued in the program towards paying the hijackers 3 BTC.

The text explained the payment instructions.

Post your sending address here:__

Pay to Bitcoin wallet

1N9SN3vAArSwYjQixuBBiTKDsNJtRgnAab

<<Click here to pay>>

Lexi typed the address into her mobile phone and continued.

Before sending 3 Bitcoins in payment, a pop-up window appeared with a new warning.

"Make sure that you enter the payment information correctly! Each incorrect attempt will reduce the time to destroy the private key in half!

Are you sure that you have entered the payment information correctly?

Press "Yes" to continue.

After pressing "Yes", Lexi saw the screen scroll down. The ransomware now read,

WAITING FOR PAYMENT ACTIVATION

Payments are processed manually after a review and can take up to 1 business day. The private key destruction is now suspended for the time of payment processing. Files will decrypt automatically after payment activation. Do not disconnect from the Internet or turn off the computer.

CryptoLocker

Relieved to have unlocked the computer Lexi now protested, "I have to wait one full day to get my work back? These jerks."

Noah interrupted her, "It is usually not that long, several guys across town had the same CryptoLocker hijack and it only took 3 hours to free up theirs. Just be glad you have the Bitcoins."

Lexi barked back to him, "Yes, lucky me."

Southeast Portland, Oregon

It was 3:00 pm on Friday and this was payday for the dozen happy employees at the Main Street Bakery. Sarina began passing out the paychecks. After each employee graciously accepted an envelope, most exited from the back of the building. Four employees remained standing in the tiny office staring at their pay slips. Sarina stood and approached the first person, "$128.84 in Bitcoin," she said as they both raised their smartphones. Sarina, scanned a QR code, then touched her phone twice. She made the payment and the first employee thanked her and left. This action was repeated three more times until the room had emptied.

Sarina had been offering all employees the opportunity to receive up to 20% of their pay in Bitcoin. So far, 4 had accepted her offer. Two of them had family in other countries and would be sending the coins home, and the other two workers used Bitcoin in everyday business, buying coffee, food or shopping online.

Sarina had set up an account at BTC-Beijing and had required anyone wishing to be paid with BTC to do the same. The company's mobile app allowed her to pay employees instantly through the BTC-Beijing account at no cost and no transaction fees. She felt strongly that this app was revolutionizing mobile payments and had hoped that BitStarter might also adopt a similar platform.

Upon enquiring with Bitstarter, she was informed that US regulations would not permit such payments. She did not fully understand the US rules and regulations surrounding Bitcoin and was also unsure about the Bitcoin payroll taxes. Luckily, Portland had no sales tax, which excluded her from yet another issue when accepting Bitcoin for retail goods. While her husband Paul had always loved and promoted Bitcoin, Sarina handled the company paperwork. She recognized some prominent future Bitcoin issues which needed to be resolved before Bitcoin would be adopted by a mainstream US audience.

Santa Clarita, California

Jan had located a large Bitcoin "exchange" firm in San Francisco, which was recommended by everyone online. It was called Bitstarter. The business allowed individuals, such as herself, to transfer money from her bank account to an online Bitstarter account and purchase Bitcoins. It was very similar to how PayPal worked. After that purchase, she could do anything she wanted with her new Bitcoins. She could even make a high yield investment. Jan created a Bitstarter account and transferred $25,000 of her PayPal funds, through her bank into the new Bitstarter account. Three days later she owned a large stack of Bitcoins, the world's next currency.

She could not be more pleased with her purchase!

After the Bitcoins had appeared in her wallet, 20,000 dollars worth of Bitcoins was transferred to the online "HYIP Trust". She had kept the extra $5,000 in the Bitcoins in the Bitstarter online wallet.

The $20,000 payment had been her first real Bitcoin transaction. At that moment, her 190-day investment clock had started ticking. In six months' time, her son would be graduating from high school and moving on to a good college of his choice. With the $50,000 return investment earned by the Trust, Jan could pay almost all of his expenses for the first two years.

Each day, for the next 190 days, a Bitcoin payment of $280 would be automatically deposited into her Bitcoin wallet. After the full 190 days, she planned to decline rolling over the investment and withdraw her original $20,000 investment.

Including the principal and interest, she calculated that would leave her something like $53,000, in total savings. This amount was more money than she could ever earn on her own.

Jan lay in bed each night thinking about the wonderful opportunities created by Bitcoin.

She had left the $5,000 worth of Bitcoins in her online wallet, she envisioned the price of Bitcoin soaring during the next six months. Rising prices would mean more profit for her BitStarter wallet account.

She thought to herself, that perhaps once her son left home for his new college, she could afford to buy a used car with some of the profits. Working with Bitcoin was very exciting!

She understood that there was no other way in the world for her to make such a substantial profit in a short period, and this fact alone had caused the Bitcoin investment to be worth the risk.

Lagos, Nigeria

Today, Mabry had hit a big score! Just hours earlier, one of his HYIPs had a new "investor" for a full $20,000 in Bitcoin. It was rare to have such a large amount from one person, but it occasionally happened.

Once the new Bitcoins had made it through the tumbler, Mabry would head down to his Nigerian friend and associate David Owani, who operated an exchange office nearby in Lagos. Mabry could sell his Bitcoin for cash and bring home a stack of Naira and even some Euros. He figured around $17,000 US dollars' worth.

The Owani family operated two digital currency exchanges, including the downtown Lagos operation and one in Port Harcourt. They were both registered with the Corporate Affairs Commission (CAC) of Nigeria, and much care was taken to ensure a positive experience for each customer. The exchanges handled Bitcoin and also Perfect Money, WebMoney, PexPay, PayPal, OkPay and other e-Currency accounts.

After Mabry had removed the Bitcoins from the tumbler, he loaded them onto his Kilachange mobile wallet and dashed out the door. The NigeriaDigital.com exchange office was less than a kilometer away.

Seattle, Washington

It had been almost three weeks since the early morning Sheriff's raid on Julia and Steven's home. No Marijuana grow operation was present in the home and no drugs of any kind were found. Neither of them even smoked. However, the new fire safe had been opened, and the officers had found 22,000 dollars in cash.

At that point in the assault, detectives were resolved to uncover something illegal and decided to confiscate all of their computers. Fortunately, the cops had left the routers, graphics boards, and the mining rigs. However, all six laptops and the desktop PC had been removed from the house, along with the cash. No charges had been filed that night by King County or any during the following three weeks.

When the Police found all the overheated computer equipment, and it was explained the couple was mining Bitcoin, there was no question why their electric bill had been so high. However, new problems had emerged based on the large amount of cash that officers had confiscated.

Julia borrowed a laptop from a friend and managed to repair their mining operation. Two weeks later, most of their mining rigs were back online earning fresh Bitcoins.

Unfortunately, the couple had been unable or unwilling to explain the $22,000 as reported income. It seemed like the government was going to keep their money.

West Africa

James had been receiving Africa Clean Water Bitcoin donations all week long and today, it was time to convert most of the Bitcoins into local usable Nigerian currency. The Naira was this country's local government money, and he could exchange one Bitcoin into more than 11,000 Naira. There were 32 Bitcoins in the charity account and on a good day; his charity could obtain about 350,000 Naira. This number was not exactly a king's ransom, but each week, the Bitcoin donations had allowed them to continue drilling new wells in much-needed areas.

Bitcoin had taken Nigeria by storm. If Mpesa was Kenya's digital currency, then Bitcoin was Nigeria's version of digital money.

The Kilachange mobile wallet facilitated all mobile Bitcoin transactions in Nigeria and beyond. Kilachange functioned well on any web enabled mobile phone and in some areas, the wallet was even integrated with Mpesa.

From Algeria to Zimbabwe, Kilachange was the tool that users needed to transact business throughout more than 50 African regions. The receiver's mobile phone number was the only piece of data required to complete a payment. Just about any size payment, denominated in "Millibits", could be sent from one phone to another.

Of course, working in Nigeria had presented many challenges such as widespread bribery and corruption. Consequently, a portion of each weekly Bitcoin payout had to be converted into local cash notes that were inevitably being used to "grease the wheels" of progress across Nigeria.

In Lagos, James and his AWC group had always exchanged a small batch of Bitcoins for cash notes through the Lagos office of NigeriaDigital.com. The digital currency exchange company was not the largest in Lagos, but the owner, David Owani, was reputable and safe. In just a few minutes of travel time, James could drop by the NigeriaDigital.com offices and use his mobile phone to sell some of the charity's Bitcoin and leave with currency in his pocket. James made this trip dozens of times throughout the year.

On a Friday afternoon in Lagos, James arrived at David's office and converted 4 Bitcoin into local currency.

As he stood talking with David, another man entered the shop carrying a small leather bag. James recognized the container as a money satchel or bank bag, which couriers in Nigeria used for transporting valuable items. David had introduced the man as Mabry and said that he was a local businessman involved in the digital currency business.

James had courteously greeted the man and exited the building beginning his long muddy cross country trip to the next ACW drilling location.

Santa Clarita, California

Jan returned home from her tutoring job late that Friday. She immediately turned on the computer and checked her Trust investment. After 14 days of receiving regular payments, Jan was shocked to see that today, her $280 interest payment had not arrived. While this was upsetting, she had worked several jobs that day and was too tired to investigate further. She climbed into bed and fell right into a deep sleep.

The next morning she arose very early and immediately turned on her computer. Her Bitcoin account showed a big zero, where the $280 daily interest payment should have appeared. She immediately tried to log onto the investment trust's website, but was denied entry. Entering her username and password the site displayed, "No such user exists."

Jan was trying to stay calm but began to panic. She thought that perhaps she had entered the wrong password. However, upon entering it again yielded the same result.

A text reading, "No such user exists," again appeared on the website.

Oh my god, she thought, what has happened to my money? Panicked and too upset to understand what was happening, she went into work and waitressed all day trying not to think about the problem. She came to the conclusion, as she boarded the bus for home, that the website had computer issues, and her money was safe.

At home, she tried accessing her funds. However, today's news was even worse. As she typed in the web domain URL, she received a blank page. Today, the entire website was missing. There was a simple text message on the screen that read, "Sorry, our accounts were hacked, and we lost all the Bitcoin."

"Oh my god," she thought, the Bitcoin money, is my $20,000 Trust investment gone? Her mind raced with questions. How could this have happened? How could she get her money back?

As she said aloud, "This is not happening." She searched the Internet for a consumer protection office within the State of California

To her surprise, on the front page of the California Department of Consumer Affairs' website, she quickly found a Bitcoin consumer warning about the risks of virtual currency. Part of the text read:

"… Those considering investing in virtual currency should know that its use may be unregulated, they are highly volatile in value, and can be stolen or subject to cyber crime."

Jan was in tears as she dialed 411 to find a phone number of the State of California consumer protection office. She connected with Department of Consumer Affairs. After a brief conversation, she was then referred to the California Consumer Services Office, Department of Business Oversight. After calling this number, Jan now reached a voice mailbox for Mr. John Koch.

She had only briefly investigated online high yielding investments and concluded that, everyone was investing in Bitcoin HYIPs, so they must be legitimate.

She had received the investment newsletter and even checked with the Bitcoin Investment monitor and rating website. Her Trust Investment had received five stars. The "Assured Bitcoin Investment Trust" held a high "investment" score on several websites, and it showed a hyperlink to the Bitcoin Business Foundation Center.

A few minutes later, Mr. Koch called her back only to explain that his department could not handle that type of complaint. He directed Jan to a recent report created by their office entitled, "What You Should Know about Bitcoin Virtual Currency."

In reference to the people who had stolen her money, she asked the sympathetic Mr. Koch, "How can they do this?"

Koch responded, "I often hear about these cases Mrs. Johnson, there is currently no federal or state regulation of offshore digital currency websites. While the State of California requires these sites to register and obtain the proper licensing, in most cases the companies don't register with the state. We cannot track down the operators before they disappear with the victim's money. An unlicensed digital currency "investment" should immediately be a 100% a red flag, not to do business with these entities. Let me ask you another question, did you refer any other "investors" to the website and receive a referral bonus?"

Jan responded, "No."

Koch continued, "Virtually all HYIP schemes require participants to use a digital currency such as Bitcoin and most pay a generous referral fee. Many victims of these investment schemes end up referring other members of their family or associates from their employment. Last year, we had an entire office of IBT Computer employees here in California that lost money through an online high yield investment. Now, Mrs. Johnson, I'm going to give you some additional contacts to report your loss. Please write these down."

http://www.stopfraud.gov/ The Financial Fraud Enforcement Task Force

http://www.ic3.gov/ The Internet Crime Complaint Center

http://www.sec.gov/ The Securities and Exchange Commission.

Quietly sobbing on the line, Jan asked, "What happened to my money? Is there any chance of getting the Bitcoin back?"

Koch replied, "Mrs. Johnson, unless the scam operators call you up, apologize and volunteer to send you a check, there is no chance to recover any of your Bitcoin funds. Mrs. Johnson, I also suggest that call FINRA at (240) 356-4957 or file a complaint using FINRA's online Investor Complaint Center."

Jan, "What is FINRA?"

He stated, "This is the Financial Industry Regulatory Authority, a part of the Federal government."

Now crying, Jan thanked Mr. Koch and abruptly ended the call.

Jan had just lost almost all of the hard earned money that she had saved over the past decade. She was heartbroken. As she planned a talk with her son, about attending the local community college, she wished she had never heard of Bitcoin. From the entire $20,000 in Bitcoin that had been "invested", just over $1,700 now remained.

Seattle, Washington

Riley had driven all the way from Portland to Seattle for this evening's Bitcoin Meetup. Accompanying him were several of the new Bitcoin ATMs he planned to operate during the Meetup. He was pleased to see that the Meetup was packed with more than 60 people and the room was buzzing with news. As he soon discovered, that morning a pair of local Bitcoin miners, who regularly attended the Meetup, had been arrested.

After asking, "What happened?" he was handed a copy of the Seattle Times. He began to read the article entitled "Seattle Bitcoin Miners Arrested in Mining Investigation".

> Authorities today charged two King County residents engaged in mining Bitcoin Convertible Virtual Currency with operating an unlicensed money transmitting business.
>
> Julia Applebaum and Steven Rogers, of Seattle, Washington, have been indicted in a one-count Indictment for violating 18 U.S.C. -SS 1960 (a) by knowingly conducting an "unlicensed money transmitting business," as defined by Section subsection (b)(1)(B) of the statute.
>
> Authorities alleged that the defendants knew of the federal registration and state licensing requirements and intentionally failed to register their status as a money services business.
>
> The couple failed to obtain a license to operate the money transmitting business from the Washington Department of

Financial Institutions, and to register as money transmitters with the United States Treasury's Financial Crime Enforcement Network ("FinCEN") as required by law.

FinCEN's Regulations for Virtual Currency Mining Operations clearly states that those mining Bitcoin as a for-profit business and transmitting those mined Bitcoin to another in exchange for monetary value, are considered to be a Money Service Business and required to register as a Money Transmitter.

The FinCEN guidance had made clear that an administrator or exchanger of convertible virtual currencies that accepts and transmits a convertible virtual currency or buys or sells convertible virtual currency in exchange for currency of legal tender or another convertible virtual currency for any reason (including when intermediating between a user and a seller of goods or services the user is purchasing on the user's behalf) is a money transmitter under FinCEN's regulations, unless a limitation to or exemption from the definition applies to the person.

The prosecutors for the State of Washington released this statement.

"Discovering financial crimes requires transparency in all types of financial transactions. We are now more determined than ever before, to bring to justice those attempting illegally to hide the movement of funds using Bitcoin Virtual Currency. Crimes such as this undermine the stability and prosperity of our great American financial system. Our undercover agents had infiltrated the illegal operation run through Mylocalbitcoins.net. Over a period of several months, the undercovers had been using cash to purchase Bitcoins illegally directly from miners here in the Seattle area."

Now released on bail, both defendants have pled not guilty. If convicted, each faces a maximum possible sentence of 5 year's imprisonment and fines of up to $250,000 each.

Court documents reveal that undercover agents had made cash purchases of Bitcoin, totaling in excess of $100,000, through local Seattle Bitcoin Meetups. Agents had also contacted individuals that were selling Bitcoin in the Seattle area through MyLocalBitcoins.net.

Earlier this year, the defendant's home had been raided by King County Sheriff's officers. During that raid, $22,000 in cash and several computers had been seized. This case is the first instance of prosecuting Bitcoin miners ever filed in the United States.

For-profit miners of convertible virtual currency, including Bitcoin, are considered money transmitters and are subject to regulations if they do substantial business in the United States. Specifically, federal regulations require a for-profit convertible virtual currency miner to register with the Department of Treasury's Financial Crimes Enforcement Network ("FinCEN") as a money service business and develop and maintain an effective AML program. Maintaining an effective AML program requires filing Suspicious Activity Reports, including reporting substantial transactions or patterns of transactions involving the use of the money service business to facilitate criminal activity. Maintaining an effective AML program also requires implementing effective means of verifying customer identities. In particular, money services businesses must, at a minimum, verify and keep a record of the identity of any customer involved in the transmission of funds larger than $3,000.

This information and more is available from the U.S. Bank Secrecy Act / Anti-Money Laundering Examination Manual. Defendants are innocent until proven otherwise.

Santa Clarita, California

Ten days after submitting her complaint, Jan received an email letter from the International Online Crime Internet Complaint Center with an official response and details about her $20,000 Bitcoin Trust investment.

Absent any formalities, it read:

> There can be little or no consumer protection when investing in an offshore, anonymous, web business. Supervision and regulation are impossible without proper state and federal licensing.
>
> There is no available information on what foreign company operated the fraudulent investment scheme and from what jurisdiction.
>
> The investment required Bitcoin convertible virtual currency; there were no traceable bank or credit card payments.
>
> The parties operating the HYIP had cloaked themselves in secrecy. Internet proxies were used to connect to the web site's server, and there was no direct electronic trail or link to any party. There was no phone number or business office address. Contact was only available through a website form.
>
> The site failed to disclose who would be acting as custodian of the investor funds.
>
> As published on the website, investor returns were allegedly generated trading Bitcoin. This activity creates a situation where Bitcoin may have functioned as an unregistered security. Please contact the Securities and Exchange Commission in Washington, DC to file a formal complaint.
>
> Please be aware of these additional issues that stem from using Bitcoin and other virtual currencies.

Virtual currency makes it very difficult to recover stolen or lost funds. Bitcoin is unlike a stolen credit card or hacked bank account. When Bitcoin funds go missing, there is virtually no trace or recovery process. If a person uses a mobile wallet and then loses the phone, that Bitcoin is not recoverable. If a user's personal computer breaks or is rendered unusable, all of the Bitcoin held in a wallet on that computer is also un-recoverable.

Bitcoin is a new emerging technology. The growth and expansion of emerging technologies can quickly render software and security measures obsolete. Regulatory agencies cannot predict future failures and issues of virtual currency systems.

The daily price and value of Bitcoin fluctuates. In the last 24 months, there have been enormous variations in Bitcoin's reported price, sometimes gaining 100% or losing 100% in a short period. This price movement can quickly lead to a loss of investment value.

Bitcoin's usage has been connected with online criminal enterprises, including illegal drug transactions, small arms trading, money laundering, and online investment fraud.

The letter ended with, "Your complaint has been received and recorded." Her hope of ever recovering any money ended with that letter.

Burbank, California

Accepting Bitcoins through a BitStarter account was just like accepting donations using any other method of payment. The account owner never handled the Bitcoin currency. Upon receipt of a Bitcoin donation, the digital currency was instantly converted into dollars and automatically deposited into the party's bank account each day.

The HTML form Raj had designed to accept donations for candidates, permitted contributions as low as $3, $5 and $10 while capping the maximum single gift at $100. A majority of those people who had generously donated Bitcoin to the party had sent in between $3 and $10. Additional detailed information on those donations showed that 95% of the Bitcoins came from supporters between the ages of 18 and 25.

For Raj, the thrilling part of Bitcoin's entry into local politics, was the demographic of the new Bitcoin voters. His research indicated that those donating Bitcoin had not been involved in past politician campaigns or even voted. The new Bitcoin micro-donation of $3-$5 dollars, which had been gaining traction in California, had also been successful in attracting brand new young voters to the Republican Party.

Raj had created an easy to install Bitcoin HTML template that accepted Bitcoin donations. Any Republican candidate could use it and begin accepting Bitcoin donations through their election or re-election website.

Raj had shown his GOP office that it was possible to attract young Republican voters using Bitcoin. This action was something that the Republican Party had not done since Richard Nixon was in office!

Bitcoin micro-donations had proven to be an inexpensive, fraud-free method of accepting donations and a successful new marketing tool for Republicans.

The Federal Government & Operation Rocket

Re: The death of Mr. Charles Martin

Earlier this year, following the receipt of detailed credit card information received from Interpol, federal agencies commenced Operation Rocket. This law enforcement action was the largest crackdown on child pornography and related computer crimes in US history.

* More than 90,000 individuals in over 22 countries were found to have accessed illegal material during the investigation

* 5,934 suspects were identified in the United States

* 4,488 search warrants were issued

* 3,089 US arrested were made

* 2,844 formal charges relating to child pornography were filed against US citizens

* 1,583 of the accused were convicted

* 243 underage children were removed from dangerous situations

* 38 of the arrested persons committed suicide during the investigation

While the federal operation was successful in identifying and prosecuting suspected pedophiles and sex offenders, many questions have arisen from the validity of the government's investigative procedures.

The homes and businesses searched during the investigation included those occupied by television celebrities, Congressmen, registered sex offenders and even the 88-year old deacon from a large church in Portland, Oregon. Serious errors on behalf of US agents and aggressive prosecutors may have resulted in many false arrests.

Later evidence presented to the court, determined that many of the credit cards linked to the purchase of child pornography were fraudulently obtained and used by unknown third parties.

At the time of their arrests, the rightful credit card owners were unaware that their information had been stolen or fraudulently used. None of these individuals were found to be in possession of any illegal evidence, such as incriminating pictures or emails on any confiscated computer or mobile device. The only evidence that had been used to prosecute many of the individuals was the single receipt for a credit card payment through the illegal website.

Due to the severity of the criminal charges which resulted from Operation Rocket, 184 young children, who had living at home with their parents or single father at the time of the arrests, were immediately removed from the households and placed into child protective services.

Prosecutors filed 2,844 formal charges relating to child pornography against US citizens. Out of that number of defendants, 1,286 cases were eventually dropped due to credit card fraud.

In more than a thousand of these cases, the defendant's credit card information was found to have been stolen from the database of a national department store. Officials from the department store's headquarters in New York City confirmed that an Eastern European hacker group had compromised the store's servers. This action resulted in the loss of more than 77 million customer's personal and financial data profiles.

The US Attorney, who had been prosecuting Charles Martin, made this statement to the press regarding Mr. Martin's suicide:

"We don't prosecute offenders based on a simple credit card charge. In the case of the late Mr. Charles Martin, our task force went to the individual's bank and confirmed that a transaction had taken place from a local web IP address. Investigators also verified that Mr. Martin had never reported his card stolen or that an unauthorized party had used the card in a fraudulent transaction."

Stolen credit card and identity information are regularly bought and sold through Internet Darknet markets and online "carder" forums. In a majority of these sales, Bitcoin is used as the anonymous form of payment for the stolen data.

Denver, Colorado

Two month after arranging Mr. Green's Bitcoin liquidation through BTC-Beijing, the Denver store chain's overall Bitcoin sales had increased more than 20%. Georgina felt like Bitcoin had really been accepted by the store's customers.

The icing on her cake was not having to pay credit card transaction fees on each sales. Without the 3%-4% cost per transaction, which credit cards were charging, the store was saving thousands of dollars each day.

Despite a rough start, Bitcoin virtual currency had become a real blessing to Mr. Green's legal marijuana business. Now other legal Marijuana vendors in Colorado were looking into accepting the virtual currency.

She even proudly displayed a framed Bitcoin original graphic on her office wall. It had been a gift from one of Mr. Green's regular customers. Under the vintage drawing of an Air Force Bomber dropping Bitcoins across the horizon, it read, "Bitcoin, not bombs." She loved it.

With the Colorado stores producing a steady profit each day, Georgina made it a point to pay off her start up loan. She wired 1.23 million dollars from the Singapore account back to her early investors. The old friends in California, who had loaned her the startup capital to open 4 stores, were happy to see the entire loan paid back with interest. She even sent some flowers to the IRS employee in Denver who had suggested the corporate work around which allowed them to pay taxes on time electronically.

Melbourne, Australia

While Expedia.com, the world's leading online travel agency, was already accepting Bitcoins for airline tickets, it was recommended to Abdul that he purchase his travel through a local Melbourne agent. His handler had told him to arrive in person, and pay for the transaction with his legal Bitcoin funded card.

Flying out of the Melbourne airport to his terrorist training, Abdul was very careful to comply with all airport regulations. He made sure that he had not brought any liquid, aerosol or gel items; he was able to move quickly through airport security screening.

As his laptop rolled out of the x-ray scanner, the security officer picked it up and instructed Abdul to turn on the machine. The officer had noticed a large QR code sticker below the keyboard as Abdul had powered up the laptop.

He asked, "What does this code represent?"

Abdul responded, "This is a QR code representing my Bitcoin wallet payment address."

The airport security officer then began pointing to Abduls' carry-on backpack and asked a very unusual question. He said, "Do you have any Bitcoins in your other luggage?"

Abdul did not understand the question. He thought to himself, "Bitcoins are digital files, not physical coins, why was the officer asking such a question?" He responded to the officer saying, "I'm sorry, I don't understand, what is the question, please?"

Again, the security officer pointed to his carry-on luggage and asked, "Bitcoins, do you have any coins packed in your luggage which you wish to disclose?"

Remembering that his Middle East associates had advised him not to engage any airport agents in discussion, Abdul simply responded, "No sir," and the officer directed him through security and onto his terminal.

Confidently walking to his plane, Abdul relished the idea that even Australian airport security personnel did not understand Bitcoins!

Denver, Colorado

Four months after Mr. Green's accepted its first Bitcoin sale, Georgina was hit with a bombshell. Overnight, the FBI and the Drug Enforcement Administration had raided and closed all four store locations. The agents had confiscated everything in the stores including cash, computers, and all the marijuana. The raid by federal agents had been part of an indictment filed under seal by a federal grand jury sitting in Denver, Colorado.

136

United States District Court, Denver Colorado

United States of America

- v. -

Mr. Green's Dispensary

Green Bitcoin Trading

Georgina Ray

18 U.S.C. § 1956 Conspiracy to Launder Monetary Instruments;

18 U.S.C. § 1960 Operation of a Unlicensed Money Transmitting Business;

26 U.S.C. § 7201 Attempt to evade or defeat tax

18 U.S.C. § 371 Conspiracy to Defraud the United States

18 U.S.C. § 982(a)(1) (Criminal Forfeiture).

The following was a press statement released by the office of the US Attorney in Denver.

Mr. Green's Dispensary Press Conference

Prepared Remarks of U.S. Attorney Norman Stevenson

Good afternoon. My name is Norman Stevenson, and I am the United States Attorney for the District of Colorado.

Today, we announce charges in what is the first federal criminal case brought against a Marijuana Dispensary licensed and operating in the State of Colorado.

Specifically, we have unsealed charges against Mr. Green's Dispensary, Green Bitcoin Trading Corporation and Ms. Georgina Ray. These included Conspiracy to Launder Monetary Instruments, Operation of an Unlicensed Money Transmitting Business, Attempt to evade or defeat tax and Conspiracy to Defraud the United States.

For the past four months, the defendants have operated a sophisticated Bitcoin money laundering scheme using a Delaware corporation, between banks in China, Singapore, and the United States.

The operation included weekly deposits, as large as $2.6 million dollars, denominated in Bitcoin. The business had transferred the funds out of the United States and exchanged Bitcoin into national currency through an unlicensed financial corporation in Beijing China. Georgina Ray then wired into third party accounts located in Singapore. From Singapore, the laundered funds were wired to US accounts including those of known associates of Georgina Ray residing in California. At least 1.23 million dollars of undeclared income was withdrawn by the defendant or "skimmed" by Ms. Ray and routed to her close associates.

Enacted as Article 18, Section 16 of the Colorado State Constitution, specially licensed businesses are now permitted to sell marijuana for recreational use. Since the first store officially opened on January 1, 2014 agencies of the federal government have been closely supervising the activity of all participants in this new industry.

Mr. Green's Bitcoin exchange banking operation was intentionally created by the defendant and structured to facilitate criminal activity by concealing Bitcoin income and disguising the source of Bitcoin funds.

Additionally, the 4 Denver area operations included unlicensed currency exchange businesses known as Bitcoin ATMS. These financial exchanges were being operated without registration or proper supervision. Millions of dollars in cash was converted each day into Bitcoins that she anonymously transferred out of the country.

As alleged, Mr. Green's deliberately operated the business in a way to encourage and attract new unreported Bitcoin customer sales and used unregulated virtual currency to conceal the unreported income.

Mr. Green's allegedly processed more than 400,000 separate Bitcoin financial transactions and laundered just over $26,000,000 in Bitcoin virtual currency proceeds through unlicensed foreign agents.

We have indicted Mr. Green's Dispensary because, as alleged, this was a sophisticated ongoing Bitcoin money laundering operation that generated millions of dollar each week. Accepting an unregulated and unsupervised method of payment such as Bitcoin allowed income to go unreported.

Also charged in the indictment for conspiracy, Ms. Georgina Ray was responsible for concealing Bitcoin income, and invisibly funneling this money out of the United States. She was observed skimming 1.23 million dollars of this income and wiring it directly into bank accounts of friends and associates in California. The defendant ultimately hid the income that flowed through Bitcoin from the Internal Revenue Service.

In addition to bringing criminal charges, today we have also effectively shut down Mr. Green's Dispensary and seized the contents of all four Denver-area store locations. The seizure included a substantial amount of Marijuana and related products. Agents also confiscated 4 Bitcoin ATM bank machines.

We have also seized $6 million of funds, and we have restrained or seized a total of 4 bank accounts around the world.

Bitcoin has quickly became a financial tool used by criminals for the movement of funds in and out of the United States. Bitcoin provides anonymity on global financial transactions; Bitcoin allowed the defendants to engage in illegal transactions with impunity. This type of commercial activity would h---ave been impossible in the regulated United States financial system.

Unlike traditional banks or legitimate credit card processing, Bitcoin does not require users to validate personal identifying information. In this case, millions of dollars' worth of Bitcoin, which moved between the US and China, needed no identification and no source of funds declaration from the sender. Bitcoin circumvents US anti-money laundering regulations.

Overseas bank accounts were opened by the defendant, Ms. Georgina Ray, under separate third party controlled corporations in order to evade detection by the Internal Revenue Service.

This prosecution by the US Attorney's Office should be a warning to all companies in the US considering Bitcoin.

The United States operates on a system of financial laws and regulations; we will not tolerate the illegal use of Bitcoin virtual currency to circumvent US regulations.

This case is one of the fastest our office has ever prosecuted, and it has been a coordinated global enforcement effort. Over the four months leading up to this indictment, the agents and our foreign partners executed many search warrants. One action included the first ever searches of a cloud server. We obtained multiple wiretaps, reviewed countless financial documents and conducted interviews.

Financial cybercrime poses a significant problem for to this country. Bitcoin virtual currency, when used by criminal organizations, threatens our national security, our economic security, and our privacy. I would like to thank our partner, in this case, the Asset Forfeiture and Money Laundering Section of the Department of Justice.

The End